Tales of Strange and Wonderful

Order this book online at www.trafford.com
or email orders@trafford.com

Most Trafford titles are also available at major online book retailers.

Printed in Victoria, BC, Canada.

ISBN: 978-1-4269-2645-7 (sc)
ISBN: 978-1-4269-2646-4 (hc)

Library Of Congress Control Number: 2010906675

*Our mission is to efficiently provide the world's finest, most comprehensive book publishing
service, enabling every author to experience success. To find out how to publish your book, your
way, and have it available worldwide, visit us online at www.trafford.com*

Trafford rev. 05/20/2010

 www.trafford.com

North America & international
toll-free: 1 888 232 4444 (USA & Canada)
phone: 250 383 6864 ♦ fax: 812 355 4082

Tales of the Strange and Wonderful

as told by

"The Ol' Turkey Hunter"

Trafford Publishing
Indianapolis, Indiana

The Ol' Turkey Hunter

Epigraph

I've got too
much to gain
to lose.

Dottie Rambo

The Ol' Turkey Hunter

ACKNOWLEDGMENTS

The influences upon this book are endless, but I'll try to acknowledge three or four of the most influential.

Thanks to the Lockman Foundation for the use of *The New American Standard Bible* verses. I found this translation to be easy reading and more understandable that some of the less contemporary translations of the Holy Bible. There would be no basis for this book without the great stories of the Holy Bible.

Thanks also to Wikipedia, the free encyclopedia. It is a source of many great pictures that are mostly available for reprinting. Hopefully, these pictures will add greatly to the understanding of the stories to follow, but the main reason for the pictures is my redneck hunting buddies. They don't read much, but they do like to look at pictures.

Good or bad, I've tried to throw some of the unique personality of The Ol' Turkey Hunter into this book. There are so many factors that go into personality development and I consider myself to be extremely lucky to have lived in the time and place where I have lived my life.

First, I was so lucky to be born to parents that were great examples of what parents should be, a family that held closely to Judeo-Christian concepts. My mom and dad spent countless hours at church, our sporting events, and 4-H meetings, any activity us kids participated in.

Next, the community also had a major impact upon my life. The Huntsville community where I grew up was kind of like Mayberry, but without Sheriff Taylor and the drunk, Otis. To me, it was as close to growing up in Paradise as anyone could possibly experience.

I remember the older men of our small community who were pillars. Men with a moral backbone, willing and able to contribute to the community, especially with their time. Kenny Marlow, Junior Toland, Mutt Roberts, Donald Melvin, Cab Drake, Bud Wright, Ansel Hare, Sterling Ambrosius, Joyce Farwell, Bob Sapp, and many, many more. They were outstanding role models for any young man.

Of course, my first wife Katie, with her perpetual positive attitude, has supported me for over 40 years now. That's a long time to put up with me. And her parents, Ed and Roma, could not have been better in-laws. Both have given me new perspectives and different outlooks on life.

And then there are the job experiences. I guess that you'd have to say that I can't keep a job. That's been like a revolving door, but as a result, I have experienced many different livelihoods and I've gotten to know thousands of people with a wide variety of backgrounds, from millionaires to welfare recipients.

One of the most rewarding jobs was working as a family representative at a private specialty boarding school. I got to supervise hundreds of troubled teens that came from all over the United States. What I learned through the programs offered by the academy and the hours of group therapy that I supervised where students "bared their souls" is the basis for "The Parable of the Turkey Hunter". "The Parable of the Turkey Hunter" is a presentation that features the tricks that turkey hunters use to destroy a turkey, and then shows the parallels of how negative forces destroy our lives, how they steal our peace, our joy, and our hope.

While counselling at the academy, I studied a book by John Bradshaw called "Healing the Shame that Binds You". This book gave me many insights into the reactions of individuals to many different situations and insights into what was causing certain behaviours in the troubled teens. I believe that with the information from this book, many troubled teens were able to heal their souls somewhat. The insights I gained there are invaluable.

Also, I would like to acknowledge and thank Rudy Kemppainen for suggesting the final title of the book.

I'm sure there are many other acknowledgements that need to be included, but if I list them all, we'll never get to the Tales of the Strange and Wonderful.

The Ol' Turkey Hunter

CONTENTS

The Ol' Turkey Hunter

Introduction

You will enjoy the stories you are about to read in this book.

David Kerr has a wholesome, mischievous humor with a creative insight reminiscent of those early homemade philosophers who have endeared themselves to American readers for over one-hundred-fifty years; although the earliest are seldom read much anymore. I'm sure that Will Rogers, Mark Twain, and other names are familiar to you still.

In these stories you will find some long-familiar themes viewed from a different perspective, which sometimes embellishes, sometimes disturbs, but will bring a smile, if not a laugh, and that you find will come back to you in your thoughts.

I discovered that if I read one chapter a day and read it early in my day, not just once, but twice or three times, I found myself revisiting it several times throughout the day. In addition, I found myself mentally carrying on a dialogue with David, with my additional interpretations, speculations, and delightful mental meanderings—some of them bordering on the bizarre.

If I may be so bold, I'd like to suggest that you consider trying the following:

First, read only one story, as early in the morning as you conveniently can.

Then, immediately, reread it, this time underlining phrases that stand out or that you'd like to stop to think about—however, don't stop and think at this reading.

Finally, read it a third time (each is short, you may already have noticed), this time stopping a minute or two to allow yourself to savor and embellish, and sometimes to write a brief note in the margin.

I believe you will find yourself, as I did, the rest of the day, relating it to events, people, and activities, and enriching your life in surprising ways. Also, I predict that after you finish the last tale, you will not only think of someone who you know would also enjoy this book, but that you will set yours carefully aside with intentions to reread it again in the near future.

Enjoy! I wish I could be with you to share your comments as you read this book.

DuWayne Furman

Tale #1

Why Tales of the Strange and Wonderful?........

as told by

"The Ol' Turkey Hunter"

Shown here speaking to a group of senior citizens at the local nursing home. The program is called "The Parable of the Turkey Hunter". DuWayne Furman, who wrote the introduction, is in the background.

The Ol' Turkey Hunter

Why Tales of the Strange and Wonderful?

When I was a kid, I didn't like vegetables. Candy was my thing. Snickers, jaw breakers, M & M's, licorice (red or black didn't matter), Cab Drake's little one-room country store had almost anything a kid could want. I remember the candy counter was about 3 ½ feet tall and three foot square. It was all glass except for the narrow, dark wooden frame around the outside, so you could look at the candy from all sides. The back of the candy counter had two sliding glass doors. I've seen Old Cab hover over the back of the counter and slide those doors open a thousand times. He had a kind of Walter Brennan quality to his voice, and a kind of a chuckle, as he would ask and make sure that you got the candy you wanted.

Drake's General Store in Huntsville, IL

Cab's store closed last winter. It was a sad occasion. The benchs out front are gone. I never did hear how much the old potbellied coal stove sold for. I spent hours and hours sitting around that old stove warming my feet and hands in the winter, listening to the old men of the community telling their stories and cracking jokes, catching up on the local news. Rick always had everyone's attention when he told a story, and when he finished, he always threw his head back to the left as he laughed. He had such enthusiasm that everyone listened intently, regardless of the story.

The windows in front are gone or different. From the park across the street, I could never hit a ball that far but Rick and Keith could bounce a long fly ball off the blacktop and take out a window. They completely took out the window upstairs and changed the plate glass window down below.

Also gone is the Huntsville Methodist Church that always stood in the background. Katie said the picture really looks bare without the church.

Ice cream suppers held at the church were the best. We had 5 gallon ice cream freezers out back of the church. It was a big deal. The women would use cream and all of the best ingredients to make the ice cream mix in the basement of the church. Then they would pass the freezer canister out through the basement window where one of the men would put it in the hand freezer and connect the handle. Crushed ice and rock salt were added to the freezer and us young kids got to crank the freezers until it started to freeze. As the ice cream froze, it got harder to turn the handle. Then, the real men took over and finished the job. Two or three older men would give it a crank to see how hard the freezer turned to confirm that it was ready.

One of the women would then come out with a pan and a spatula to pull the mixing paddles out and seal the container in preparation for the supper that night. We were like flies on that pan of drippings. Everyone had a spoon as we fought like pigs around a slop bucker to scoop up as much of that rich, real cream delicacy as we could get. I think my buddy Dave calls that competitive feeding.

Memories are a strange thing. It's hard to understand why tears are running down my face as I'm writing this. I guess that's a really good thing, I'm very lucky to have such memories.

Photo by Author

Cab was also my bus driver in elementary school. Huntsville Grade School. I'm always proud to tell people that I graduated in the top 5 of my class, but then there is usually someone around to ruin it by adding that there were only 5 in my class. Terry, Richard, Sandy, Romel, and me. We had first, second, and third grade in the same room with the same teacher. That was actually a wonderful educational system. When you were in first grade, you got to preview what was being taught to second and third graders, and when you were in third grade, you got to review what you missed in first and second grades. And the teacher not only knew you, but she also knew your parents and your grandparents.

There weren't many discipline problems in our little school. Rarely the ping pong paddle was used, but the usual correction was administered immediately by the teacher. It consisted of the teacher grabbing the student who needed correction; one hand on his upper arm and the other hand around his wrist, and then a series of about 10 good shakes, as the student's head bounced back and forth like a rag doll. About one good shaking a month kept everyone in line.

I never did get a shaking, but once in third grade I saw two classmates quietly roll back their shirt-sleeves and compare

Huntsville Grade school
Like many other things in Huntsville, Illinois, the old school is gone. It had three classrooms and a lunchroom. Two swing sets with a slide and two titer-totters were on the left of the school and the

gravel basketball court was on the right of the school as pictured here.

Photo by author.

how big their arm muscles were. Well, I was not about to be outdone, so I made a big muscle myself (at least as big as a third grader can) to show that I was strong too. Well, the teacher saw this little exhibition and we were in trouble. Our punishment was that all three of us had to stand in front of all of the first, second, and third graders, roll up our sleeves, and show off our muscles. That was a really bad thing. I went home and told my dad that night, half expecting a whipping, but he said that when he was a kid he had to stand in front of the class and pull his ears and stick out his tongue. I guess that he sympathized with me a little bit and let me off the hook.

One boy that moved away before eighth grade had a problem of wetting his pants at school. He was the one who usually got the shaking, but when that didn't work, I remember him having to wear a big white diaper over his dark blue overalls. Boy was I glad that I never peed my pants.

Let's see, I was talking about Cab. When I got older, I got up the nerve to ask Cab how he got his nickname. Apparently at Halloween time, the kids in the neighborhood would trick-or-treat, and usually tricked even if they got a treat. A popular trick for Cab was to take old rotten cabbages left over in the gardens from the previous summer and stuff them in the two-hole outhouses in town.

I don't suppose many people reading this have ever cleaned out an out house, but if you haven't, you can't really appreciate it. An outhouse doesn't just flush automatically. The addition of stinking old cabbage stuffed down the old two-holer would make it necessary to clean more often. . Obviously, that's a pretty funny trick, stuffing cabbage down the old 2-holer. The only trouble was, while Cab was inside doing the stuffing, the other boys trick was to tip over the outhouse. Well, it's hard to open the door of an outhouse when the structure is lying on the door. I'm not exactly sure how it all happened, and it could get pretty graphic, but the name Cab is short for Cabbage.

WPA Outhouse
This was the Cadillac of outhouses; cement floor and probably custom corn cobs.
(Courtesy Wikipedia/Wikimedia) [1]

Cooked cabbage. Yuck!!!! That brings me back to not liking vegetables. My mom said that she was not going to have a picky kid. Well, that's exactly what she got. She would shove peas down my throat, and I'd puke them right back up. She knew what was good for me, but I was too bull headed to try what I thought I wasn't going to like. But Mom was right, because I became overweight and now have type 2 diabetes from eating too much candy and not a good balance of nutritious foods (peas, carrots, spinach, broccoli, yuck!!!!!).

Hooper-Bowler-Hillstrom House

This is an interesting piece of architecture, a 2 story outhouse. It's so fancy that I bet it has customized corn cobs. My father-in-law was from Missouri and he called them "bung fodder". I'll let you figure that out. But this 2-story outhouse raises many questions and images in my mind. First, what would you call it? A 2X2? A double deuce (whoops, that was an accident, whoops again), a twin double, a double twin, an over-under? I suspect that the owners of this property are also turkey hunters.

And the logistics. Do you suppose the holes are lined up in the top and bottom of the facility? Would it be good outhouse etiquette to wait until the lower unit was evacuated before using the upper unit or does the user of the bottom unit have to fend for himself? I have known some little boys that would love a chance to use the upper facility if there was someone in the bottom. And this is really terrible. There's probably no need for pictures on the wall of the bottom unit.

(Courtesy Wikipedia/Wikimedia)[2]

All of this to try to answer the question, why Tales of the Strange and Wonderful? It used to be that almost everyone knew the popular stories of the Bible. David saved Israel from the giant Goliath, Noah took pairs of all of the animals on his ark to avoid the flood, and

Zacchaeus, well, he was a wee little man, and a wee little man was he. These are all nice stories that are fun to tell and they have a good message for us.

However, in Luke 4:4, the Bible says, *"Man shall not live by bread alone, but by every word of God."* It doesn't say "Man shall not live by bread alone, but by the <u>nice</u> words of God", it says <u>every</u> word. There are 66 books in the Bible with 1189 chapters and 31,173 verses, and although all of them have a big meaning in our lives, many of them are not well known and several are avoided as taboo. So to grow spiritually, we need to know and understand <u>all</u> of the stories of the Bible, not just the feel-good stories.

And the Israelites did not live by the word of God. Time after time after time they would forget or ignore the covenant they made with God and time after time after time they would incur the wrath of God because of either their ignorance or insubordination or greed or desire to be like other pagan nations or something.

I think a lot of people are under the impression that God's laws are a punishment or a threat. When I buy a new car, I get an owner's manual. It tells me when to change the oil and the best tire pressure and when to change the spark plugs, etc. The creator of the car knows what is good for the vehicle and the owner's manual tells me how to get the most out of that new vehicle. And if we don't take care of the maintenance, there are consequences that we won't like, like "blowing up" the engine.

We need to realize that the Bible is an owner's manual for the human race. The Creator of humans knows what is best for his creation, and the Bible tells us how to get the most out of our lives. If we ignore these guidelines, or don't even know what these guidelines are, we are much more likely to "blow up" our lives.

There are many bizarre stories found in the Bible, and some of them are avoided by the feel-good pastors of today. They are not comfortable stories to tell, nor are they politically correct, but we need to know them and understand them so that we can understand our lives and what is going on in the world today. At the end of each short story is a reference of where to find the original story in the Bible. So, here are the Tales of the Strange and Wonderful.

The Ol' Turkey Hunter

Tale #2
God's Sense of Humor

as told by

"The Ol' Turkey Hunter"

Shown here with brother, Bob, and sister, Donna (the one picking her nose) in a family Christmas Card about 1960. When I called my sister, Donna, on Sunday morning to ask her if I could use this picture, she said that she was SO glad that Mom decided to use that picture on the family Christmas card. I asked her a second time "for sure" because this could make her a very famous booger picker.

Don, Doris, David, Bobby & Donna.

The Ol' Turkey Hunter

God's Sense of Humor

When I think of God, the image of a dignified old man in a brilliant white robe with a long beard and long, flowing white hair comes to mind. I suppose that is because of the paintings of God that I've seen. The Bible says that we are created in God's image, so it makes sense to physically portray God in that manner. But what about other characteristics? Millions of people laugh at Lucille Ball and Jerry Lewis and Larry the Cable Guy. So, did we get our sense of humor from our Creator as well? I think this short story will give us some insight.

When I first put this chapter together, I found a great painting of God, exactly the way I imagine him to look. However, when I went back to find that painting and get permission to use that picture, I absolutely couldn't find it anywhere, so, maybe God didn't want to be pictured or stereotyped by me or anyone else, so you fill in the blank.
Photo by author.

Many years ago, a man named Abraham was one of God's favorite persons on Earth. God loved Abraham and promised to make his family very large and powerful. And he promised to give Abraham's

27

family a lot of choice land with great, walled cities. The only problem was, the land currently belonged to another clan, and they thought that it was their land. So there was constant fighting between Abraham's family, the Israelites, and the people already living on the land, the Canaanites.

As long as the Israelites were obedient to God, He would fight for them and defeat the Philistines, giving the Promised Land to Abraham's family. But the Israelites were rebellious, they did things their own way, and didn't do what God had instructed them to do. So eventually God quit fighting for Abraham's family and they were defeated at Ebenezer.

Well, the Israelites had an "ace in the hole", the Ark of the Covenant. A few years earlier, God gave Moses two stone tablets that contained the "Ten Commandments". I think maybe this is where the phrase "Written in Stone" comes from. But these ten rules were a contract between God and his chosen people, and since the Israelites were nomadic and didn't have a safety deposit box at the bank, they needed a place to keep this valuable contract.

So God gave Moses instructions to make the "Ark of the Covenant" as a holy place to keep the stone tablets, and also God would live there in the Ark. I think this ark is the same ark that Harrison Ford kept looking for in Indiana Jones.

I've heard many times that "if God is with us, who can be against us". So if I were losing a fight and I could bring God in on my side, that's a no brainer. And that's just what the Israelites did, they took the Ark of the Covenant to the front of the battle lines to win the war for them. But because of the rebellious nature of the Israelites, God would not help them win the battle. So guess what, the Philistines captured the Holy Ark of the Covenant. Here's how the Bible tells it.

> Thus the word of Samuel came to all Israel. Now Israel went out to meet the Philistines in battle and camped beside Ebenezer while the Philistines camped in Aphek. The Philistines drew up in battle array to meet Israel. When the battle spread, Israel was defeated before the Philistines who killed about four thousand men on the battlefield.

Ark of covenant

Wikipedia says, "A late 19th-century artist's conception of the Ark of the Covenant, employing a Renaissance cassone for the Ark and cherubim as latter-day Christian angels."

Besides the stone tablets with the ten commandments, the ark of the covenant also contained a sample of manna and Aaron's rod.

(Courtesy Wikipedia/Wikimedia)[3]

When the people came into the camp, the elders of Israel said, "Why has the LORD defeated us today before the Philistines? Let us take to ourselves from Shiloh the ark of the covenant of the LORD, that it may come among us and deliver us from the power of our enemies." So the people sent to Shiloh, and from there they carried the ark of the covenant of the LORD of hosts who sits above the cherubim; and the two sons of Eli, Hophni and Phinehas, were there with the ark of the covenant of God.

As the ark of the covenant of the LORD came into the camp, all Israel shouted with a great shout, so that the earth resounded. When the Philistines heard the noise of the shout, they said, "What does the noise of this great shout in the camp of the Hebrews mean?"

Then they understood that the ark of the LORD had
come into the camp.

The Philistines were afraid, for they said, "God
has come into the camp." And they said, "Woe to us!
For nothing like this has happened before. Woe to us!
Who shall deliver us from the hand of these mighty
gods? These are the gods who smote the Egyptians
with all kinds of plagues in the wilderness."

"Take courage and be men, O Philistines, or
you will become slaves to the Hebrews, as they have
been slaves to you; therefore, be men and fight." So the
Philistines fought and Israel was defeated, and every
man fled to his tent; and the slaughter was very great,
for there fell of Israel thirty thousand foot soldiers.

And the ark of God was taken; and the two
sons of Eli, Hophni and Phinehas, died.

This was a sobering turn of events for Israel. It appeared that
God had deserted them. It was like he had given his favor to the
Philistines. The Philistines now possessed the Ark of the Covenant,
God's home.

Now, with the Ark in Ashdod, things start getting interesting.
Israel historically had worshiped the God of Abraham, Isaac, and
Jacob, while the Philistines worshiped Dagon and other gods made of
wood and stone. So the Ark of the Covenant, God's home, ended up
in the same building as a big statue of the Philistine god, Dagon. Now
God doesn't tolerate false idols very well. That's the 2nd
commandment, and now God was in the presence of a wooden idol.
What happened next makes you wonder about the movie, "A Night at
the Museum". During the night, the wooden statue of Dagon
somehow fell face down inside the temple on the floor in front of the
ark. Hmmmmm. Sounds kind of like "every knee shall bow". Let's see
how the Bible puts it.

Now the Philistines took the ark of God and
brought it from Ebenezer to Ashdod. Then the
Philistines took the ark of God and brought it to the
house of Dagon and set it by Dagon.

When the Ashdodites arose early the next morning, behold, Dagon had fallen on his face to the ground before the ark of the LORD So they took Dagon and set him in his place again. But when they arose early the next morning, behold, Dagon had fallen on his face to the ground before the ark of the LORD. And the head of Dagon and both the palms of his hands were cut off on the threshold; only the trunk of Dagon was left to him.

I think that was God's way of saying, "not in My presence".

But earlier I asked about God's sense of humor. He is always portrayed as being so sober and serious. But in my mind's eye, I see God having a smile on his face and a little chuckle with the next turn of events.

Semitic god Dagon
(Courtesy Wikipedia/Wikimedia)[4]

The Ark of the Covenant was in the possession of the Philistines at a city called Ashdod. Mysteriously, many people and the rulers broke out with a bad case of hemorrhoids. Most people would probably tell you that there's no such thing as a "good" case of hemorrhoids. The people panicked and finally they said, "The God of Israel did this. He is the One who caused all this trouble for us and our god Dagon. We've got to get rid of this chest."

So the people of Ashdod sent the Ark of the Covenant to the city of Gath. The people of Gath also got hemorrhoids after the ark arrived. They already knew what had happened in Ashdod, so they wanted to get rid of the ark as soon as possible. So, like a hot potato, they sent the ark to the city of Ekron.

So would you be happy to accept the gift of an ark made of gold?..... if you knew it was going to give you hemorrhoids? The people of Ekron didn't want it either.

So they sent the Ark of God to Ekron. And as the ark of God came to Ekron the Ekronites cried out, saying, "They have brought the ark of the God of Israel around to us, to kill us and our people." They sent therefore and gathered all the lords of the Philistines and said, "Send away the ark of the God of Israel, and let it return to its own place, so that it will not kill us and our people." For there was a deadly confusion throughout the city; the hand of God was very heavy there. And the men who did not die were smitten with tumors and the cry of the city went up to heaven. Now the ark of the LORD had been in the country of the Philistines seven months. And the Philistines called for the priests and the diviners, saying, "What shall we do with the ark of the LORD? Tell us how we shall send it to its place." They said, "If you send away the ark of the God of Israel, do not send it empty; but you shall surely return to Him a guilt offering. Then you will be healed and it will be known to you why His hand is not removed from you."

Then they said, "What shall be the guilt offering which we shall return to Him?" And they said, "Five golden tumors and five golden mice according to the number of the lords of the Philistines, for one plague was on all of you and on your lords. So you shall make likenesses of your tumors and likenesses of your mice that ravage the land, and you shall give glory to the God of Israel; perhaps He will ease His hand from you, your gods, and your land.

I have to giggle when I think about this. Golden hemorrhoids. Sounds like a high school art class, or maybe a Broadway musical. But then the priests of Dagon proceeded to warn and instruct them,

Bullock cart in Tamil Nadu still in use in year 2009
(Courtesy Wikipedia/Wikimedia)[5]

"Why then do you harden your hearts as the Egyptians and Pharaoh hardened their hearts? When He had severely dealt with them, did they not allow the people to go, and they departed? **(Referring to the ten plagues that fell upon Egypt before Moses was allowed to lead the Israelites out of Egypt and across the Red Sea)**

Now therefore, take and prepare a new cart and two milch cows on which there has never been a yoke; and hitch the cows to the cart and take their calves home, away from them. Take the ark of the LORD and place it on the cart; and put the articles of gold which you return to Him as a guilt offering in a box by its side. Then send it away that it may go. Watch, if it goes up by the way of its own territory to Beth-shemesh, then He has done us this great evil. But if not, then we will know that it was not His hand that struck us; it happened to us by chance."

This advice was actually very good. It was smart to send a gift acknowledging their problems to God and almost genius to hook two momma cows that had never been used to pull a plow, up to a cart to watch what they did. I say that because a momma cow is very protective of her baby. They had to fight off coyotes or wild dogs that want to eat the calves. And the cows wanted the calves to nurse so the pressure of the milk in their udder didn't start causing them pain. Once a cow claims a calf, they take care of it.

Then the men did so, and took two milch cows and hitched them to the cart, and shut up their calves at home. They put the ark of the LORD on the cart, and the box with the golden mice and the likenesses of their tumors. And the cows took the straight way in the direction of Beth-shemesh; they went along the highway, lowing **(mooing or calling to their babies)** as they went, and did not turn aside to the right or to the left. And the lords of the Philistines followed them to the border of Beth-shemesh.

When we weaned calves that we raised on the farm, the cows were penned up in one lot and the calves were penned up in another lot so they could not get back together. They would desperately bawl (moo or low) for a couple of days until they decided that it was a futile effort and the pain of separation started to ease.

34

Cow and Calf
(Courtesy Wikipedia/Wikimedia)[6]

So for a momma cow to leave her baby, who is crying for her, and for her to call to her baby as she walked directly away, it was obvious to the Philistines that a supernatural power was at work. It became obvious to them that all of this grief was brought upon themselves when they took the Ark of the Covenant.

> Now the people of Beth-shemesh were reaping their wheat harvest in the valley, and they raised their eyes and saw the ark and were glad to see it. The cart came into the field of Joshua the Beth-shemite and stood there where there was a large stone; and they split the wood of the cart and offered the cows as a burnt offering to the LORD.

The Israelites were euphoric that the Ark of the Covenant had come home. The old saying "You don't know what you've got 'till it's gone" definitely applied here. This seems to be another case of God showing his chosen people that there were consequences involved when they broke their covenant with Him. This is how God drove that point home.

To go back to the beginning of the story, you need to know about Eli. Eli is the name of a priest of Shiloh, and one of the last Israelite judges before the rule of kings in ancient Israel, King Saul being the first. Eli had become old and fat as some inactive men become.

The sons of Eli, Hophni and Phinehas, meanwhile, were behaving wickedly, for example by taking for themselves all the prime cuts of meat from sacrifices, and by having sex with the women who served at the sanctuary entrance. Despite Eli's castigation of their behavior, the sons continued, and so, a "man of God" prophesied to Eli that Eli and his family would be punished for this, with all men dying "by the sword" (violently) before reaching old age.

Now a man of Benjamin (**Benjamin was one of the sons of Jacob and one of the tribes of Israel**) ran from the battle line and came to Shiloh the same day with his clothes torn and dust on his head. When he came, behold, Eli was sitting on his seat by the road eagerly watching, because his heart was trembling for the ark of God. So the man came to tell it in the city, and all the city cried out. When Eli heard the noise of the outcry, he said, "What does the noise of this commotion mean?" Then the man came hurriedly and told Eli.

Now Eli was ninety-eight years old, and his eyes were set so that he could not see. The man said to Eli, "I am the one who came from the battle line. Indeed, I escaped from the battle line today." And he said, "How did things go, my son?" Then the one who brought the news replied, "Israel has fled before the Philistines and there has also been a great slaughter among the people, and your two sons also, Hophni and Phinehas, are dead, and the ark of God has been taken." When he mentioned the ark of God, Eli fell off the seat backward beside the gate, and his neck was broken and he died, for he was old and heavy. Thus he judged Israel forty years.

The Headless Horseman Pursuing Ichabod Crane. oil
John Quidor (1801-1881)
(Courtesy Wikipedia/Wikimedia)[7]

Now his daughter-in-law, Phinehas's wife, was pregnant and about to give birth; and when she heard the news that the ark of God was taken and that her father-in-law and her husband had died, she kneeled down and gave birth, for her pains came upon her. And about the time of her death the women who stood by her said to her, "Do not be afraid, for you have given birth to a son." But she did not answer or pay attention. And she called the boy Ichabod, saying, "The glory has departed from Israel," because the ark of God was taken and because of her father-in-law and her husband.

I didn't know that Ichabod, like many names, was a Bible name and had Biblical meanings. I always thought that Ichabod was just a funny name in the Headless Horseman, but I'm sure that it was selected upon the history of the name. So to end the story,

> She said, "The glory has departed from Israel, for the ark of God was taken."

It seems that many times we only learn our lessons in the school of *really hard* knocks. And that was the case during this battle. The problem is that one generation learns the lesson but doesn't teach that lesson to the next generation, if it is taught, it isn't learned very well. So the hard knock lessons have to be learned all over again.

The happy ending to a sad story is that the Ark of the Covenant was returned to Israel and taken to several cities before it finally ended up in Solomon's temple in Jerusalem. At each stop, the cities prospered greatly while the ark was in their possession, exactly the opposite effect that was felt in the Philistine cities.

There was a lot more involved when the Israelites lost the Ark, but this part of the story gives us several insights about the God of Israel. To read the original version of this story, turn to 1 Samuel, chapters 1 thru 6.

Tale #3
Fire in the Sky

as told by

"The Ol' Turkey Hunter"

Shown here is the turkey hunter's bathtub at the first house we lived in after we got married. Katie wrote this by the picture in an old scrapbook. "This was our own personal bathtub for the summer. We took a lot of baths in it + we didn't even mind. Course we had to watch for cars."

The Ol' Turkey Hunter

Fire in the Sky

This book is about bizarre stories in the Bible, and Elijah may be the poster child, Mr. Bizarro. Well, Mr. Bizarro, Elijah, hooked up with a really wild couple, King Ahab and Queen Jezebel. To this day, for a woman to be called a Jezebel is not a good thing. Here's what AboutBibleProphecy.com had to say.

"Ahab was the seventh King of Israel. He reigned for 22 years (871-852 BC). He was the son of Omri. He married Jezebel, daughter of Ethbaal, the king of the Sidonians. Ahab, under Jezebel's influence, built a pagan temple, and allowed idols into Samaria. Elijah the prophet warned Ahab that the country would suffer from drought if the cult of Baal was not removed from the land of Israel.

Cropped screenshot of Bette Davis
from the trailer for the film *Jezebel*.
(Courtesy Wikipedia/Wikimedia)[8]

Jezebel was evil and influential. The prophets Elijah and Elisha blamed Jezebel more than Ahab for the persecution of God's prophets during that era. Jezebel's daughter, Athaliah, became Queen of Judah, and she too was evil."

Wikipedia says "The name *Jezebel* has come down through the centuries to be used as a general name for wicked women. Her Biblical account depicts her as a scheming, manipulative woman who did more than anyone to promote an evil religion. Thus, in Christian tradition, a comparison to Jezebel suggests that a person is a pagan or an apostate masquerading as a servant of God, who by manipulation and/or seduction misleads the saints of God into sins of idolatry and sexual immorality, sending them to hell.

In particular, Jezebel has come to be associated with promiscuity. The phrase "painted Jezebel", with connotations of immorality and prostitution, is based on 2 Kings 9:30-33), where Jezebel puts on her makeup just before being killed. (She may have done this to encourage her captors to keep her alive as a consort rather than kill her.) While the Bible generally depicts Jezebel as a faithful wife, she is remembered more for her introduction of Baal worship and its accompanying promiscuity to the Israelites.

While Jezebel's sexual image often has a negative connotation, some embrace it, as is evidenced by various lingerie designs named after Jezebel.

In modern usage, the name of Jezebel is sometimes used as a synonym for sexually promiscuous and sometimes controlling women, as in the title of the 1938 Bette Davis film *Jezebel* or the 1951 Frankie Laine hit "Jezebel"."

It seems that Jezebel didn't much like the prophets of God, so, she had them all killed. Like a lot of the people in the world today, she didn't like to be criticized for her actions, but she was in a position of power and she just didn't put up with it. If someone tells Donald Trump he's doing something wrong, he says, "You're Fired". Jezebel says, "You're Dead".

To catch up with this story, Ahab was a very evil king and God sent the prophet Elijah to show him the error of his ways. To show Ahab that Elijah truly was speaking for God, Elijah promised a drought until God decided to send rain, so the drought lasted three years.

Picture of drought
This is pretty extreme, but when there are big cracks in the ground, you know that the crops are suffering from heat and drought. In rich farmland, this type of cracking only occurs in the bottom of water puddles that have dried up, or at least I've never seen it this bad in a cornfield before.
(Courtesy Wikipedia/Wikimedia)[9]

You can get most people's attention with a two month drought. I remember back in 1983 and some other years when the crops all dried up in western Illinois. In '83, a farmer could put a whole field of corn in one wagon. Two to five bushels per acre, a total disaster. About the middle of July, farmers and towns people were gathering at churches and parks and praying for rain. People would try anything. Not so many years ago, they would try seeding clouds to get some moisture to fall.

Wikipedia says "Cloud seeding, a form of weather modification, is the attempt to change the amount or type of precipitation that falls from clouds, by dispersing substances into the air that serve as cloud condensation or ice nuclei, which alter the microphysical processes within the cloud. The usual intent is to increase precipitation (rain or snow), but hail and fog suppression are also widely practiced in airports. The most common chemicals used for cloud seeding include silver iodide and dry ice (frozen carbon dioxide). The jury is still out, but man's intervention into the weather has been minimal to date."

Cloud Seeding
(Courtesy Wikipedia/Wikimedia)[10]

Today, water is piped in from wells and rivers, maybe 50 miles away or more. And better than that, bottled water is available at any store or gas station in the country.

Americans take so much for granted. I bought a farm when I was 24, but that's another story. On that farm, there was a drilled well east of the house, a cistern north of the house, a drilled well and a dug well between the house and the barn, a drilled well south of the barn, a huge cistern between the barn and the south well, and a drilled well north of the north barn. With all of those wells on the farm, you would think that we had lots of water, but actually, we could either take showers and water the pigs; or take showers and wash clothes; or water the pigs and wash clothes. The reason there were so many wells was because none of them had any water, and the previous owner just kept looking.

Finally the Clayton-Camp Point Water District laid a water line past our house. I told my wife Katie that when we got city water that I was just going to flush the stool and flush the stool and flush the stool. And when we got city water after about twenty years, that's just what I did. People in western Illinois are pretty hard up for entertainment when they get their jollies watching the water swirl in a toilet.

While I'm on the subject of toilets, when I was a kid, a lot of times I would hear people say, "---- fire and save matches". I'm not just exactly sure what that meant, but I suspect that it involved hot peppers and meant something personal to each person who said it. But there were no matches involved in this story of Elijah. Let's check it out.

Clayton camp point water tower
Photo by Author

Now it happened after many days that the word of the LORD came to Elijah in the third year **(of the drought)**, saying, "Go, show yourself to Ahab, and I will send rain on the face of the earth." So Elijah went to show himself to Ahab. Now the famine was severe in Samaria. Ahab called Obadiah who was over the household (Now Obadiah feared the LORD greatly; for when Jezebel destroyed the prophets of the LORD, Obadiah took a hundred prophets and hid them by fifties in a cave, and provided them with bread and water.)

Then Ahab said to Obadiah, "Go through the land to all the springs of water and to all the valleys; perhaps we will find grass and keep the horses and mules alive, and not have to kill some of the cattle." So they divided the land between them to survey it; Ahab went one way by himself and Obadiah went another way by himself.

Now as Obadiah was on the way, behold, Elijah met him, and he recognized him and fell on his face and said, "Is this you, Elijah my master?" He said to him, "It is I. Go, say to your master, 'Behold, Elijah is here.'" He (Obadiah) said, "What sin have I committed, that you are giving your servant into the hand of Ahab to put me to death? As the LORD your God lives, there is no nation or kingdom where my master has not sent to search for you; and when they said, 'He is not here,' he (King Ahab) made the kingdom or nation swear that they could not find you. "And now you are saying, 'Go, say to your master, "Behold, Elijah is here."' It will come about when I leave you that the Spirit of the LORD will carry you where I do not know; so when I come and tell Ahab and he cannot find you, he will kill me, although I your servant have feared the LORD from my youth. Has it not been told to my master what I did when Jezebel killed the prophets of the LORD, that I hid a hundred prophets of the LORD by fifties in a cave, and provided them with bread and water? And now you are saying, 'Go, say to your master, "Behold, Elijah is here"'; he will then kill me."

Elijah said, "As the LORD of hosts lives, before whom I stand, I will surely show myself to him today." So Obadiah went to meet Ahab and told him; and Ahab went to meet Elijah. When Ahab saw Elijah, Ahab said to him, "Is this you, you troubler of Israel?" He (Elijah) said, "I have not troubled Israel, but you and your father's house have, because you have forsaken the commandments of the LORD and you have followed the Baals. Now then send and gather to me all Israel at Mount Carmel, together with 450 prophets of Baal and 400 prophets of the Asherah, who eat at Jezebel's table." So Ahab sent a message among all the sons of Israel and brought the prophets together at Mount Carmel.

Elijah came near to all the people and said, "How long will you hesitate between two opinions? If the LORD is God, follow Him; but if Baal, follow him." But the people did not answer him a word. Then Elijah said to the people, "I alone am left a prophet of the LORD, but Baal's prophets are 450 men. Now let them give us two oxen; and let them choose one ox for themselves and cut it up, and place it on the wood, but put no fire under it; and I will prepare the other ox and lay it on the wood, and I will not put a fire under it.

"Then you call on the name of your god, and I will call on the name of the LORD, and the God who answers by fire, He is God." And all the people said, "That is a good idea." So Elijah said to the prophets of Baal, "Choose one ox for yourselves and prepare it first for you are many, and call on the name of your god, but put no fire under it."

Then they took the ox which was given them and they prepared it and called on the name of Baal from morning until noon saying, "O Baal, answer us." But there was no voice and no one answered. And they leaped about the altar which they made. It came about at noon, that Elijah mocked them and said, "Call out with a loud voice, for he is a god; either he is occupied or gone aside, or is on a journey, or perhaps he is asleep and needs to be awakened."

So they cried with a loud voice and cut themselves according to their custom with swords and lances until the blood gushed out on them. When midday was past, they raved until the time of the offering of the evening sacrifice; but there was no voice, no one answered, and no one paid attention.

Then Elijah said to all the people, "Come near to me." So all the people came near to him. And he repaired the altar of the LORD which had been torn down. Elijah took twelve stones according to the number of the tribes of the sons of Jacob, to whom the word of the LORD had come, saying, "Israel shall be your name." So with the stones he built an altar in the name of the LORD, and he made a trench around the altar, large enough to hold two measures of seed. Then he arranged the wood and cut the ox in pieces and laid it on the wood. And he said, "Fill four pitchers with water and pour it on the burnt offering and on the wood." And he said, "Do it a second time," and they did it a second time. And he said, "Do it a third time," and they did it a third time. The water flowed around the altar and he also filled the trench with water.

At the time of the offering of the evening sacrifice, Elijah the prophet came near and said, "O LORD, the God of Abraham, Isaac and Israel, today let it be known that You are God in Israel and that I am Your servant and I have done all these things at Your word. Answer me, O LORD, answer me, that this people may know that You, O LORD, are God, and that You have turned their heart back again."

Then the fire of the LORD fell and consumed the burnt offering and the wood and the stones and the dust, and licked up the water that was in the trench.

When all the people saw it, they fell on their faces; and they said, "The LORD, He is God; the LORD, He is God."

Then Elijah said to them, "Seize the prophets of Baal; do not let one of them escape." So they seized them; and Elijah brought them down to the brook Kishon, and slew them there.

Now Elijah said to Ahab, "Go up, eat and drink; for there is the sound of the roar of a heavy shower." So Ahab went up to eat and drink.

An August 23, 2003 thunderstorm in Toronto, Ontario,
Canada Author John R. Southern
I always think of fire from heaven being in the form of
lightning, but I'm not sure. Check out the tree that was struck
by lightning (below).
(Courtesy Wikipedia/Wikimedia)[11]

Hardwood tree exploded when lighting strike heated sap into
steam.

When trees are struck by lightning, they usually explode when the liquid sap expands as it is heated and turned into a gas, steam. When I went out to one of my tree stands last fall, I noticed that the tree my stand was in had been struck by lightning. I wonder if the metal stand in the tree attracted the lightning?

(Courtesy Wikipedia/Wikimedia)[12]

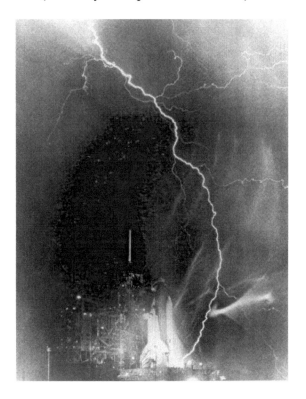

KENNEDY SPACE CENTER, FLA. - A powerful electrical storm created an eerie tapestry of light in the skies near Space Shuttle Launch Complex 39A in the hours preceding the launch of Challenger on mission STS-8 at 2:32 a.m. EDT today. Driving rains and the dazzling lightning display ceased after this photograh was taken by a remote camera set up by Sam Walton of United Press International and mission officials were able to proceed with the launch.

Lightning could dry up the water around the altar, but how could it burn up rocks if it didn't even affect the Space Shuttle which was full of rocket fuel? Maybe Elijah's fire from heaven was a little more than just lightning.

(Courtesy Wikipedia/Wikimedia)[13]

> But Elijah went up to the top of Carmel; and he crouched down on the earth and put his face between his knees. He said to his servant, "Go up now, look toward the sea." So he **(the servant)** went up and looked and said, "There is nothing." And he **(Elijah)** said, "Go back" seven times. It came about at the seventh time, that he said, "Behold, a cloud as small as a man's hand is coming up from the sea." And he **(Elijah)** said, "Go up, say to Ahab, 'Prepare your chariot and go down, so that the heavy shower does not stop you.'"
>
> In a little while the sky grew black with clouds and wind, and there was a heavy shower. And Ahab rode and went to Jezreel. Then the hand of the LORD was on Elijah, and he girded up his loins and outran Ahab to Jezreel.

I think Jezebel missed out on all of the excitement. Boy, I bet she was ticked. 450 of her priests were killed all at the same time. I bet she was stunned and furious. For some reason, the 72 year old grandmother who got tazared down in Texas comes to mind. If there was an extraordinary reason for her actions, I apologize for the following statements, but if not, I'll stand by them.

On the Today show, they showed a clip of a state patrolman who stopped a lady driving a white pickup truck for speeding in a work zone. The patrolman's dashboard video camera recorded what happened. It sure appeared that she just had a fit right there on the interstate. She was stomping around, endangering both the patrolman

and herself when the patrolman physically blocked her from stepping out into the oncoming lanes of traffic. Instead of realizing that he may have saved her life, she threw a fit about him bumping her to keep her out of traffic. I don't remember the exact words, but something like, "Oh, so you're going to bump me!!!" It was obvious to me that she was out of control. Finally the officer warned her, but when she continued her animated rave, he smacked her with his tazer. This probably isn't nice, but I actually thought that it was kind of funny to hear her wails while she was on the ground after getting tazed, "Ohhhhh, Woooooooo, Oooooooooo!!!!!"

Lots of people in the media had a fit about a young, strong officer tazing an old grandma, but what options did he have. If he'd placed his hands on her, that's a lawsuit, if she gets hit and killed on the road, that's a lawsuit, and the tazer, well, that's probably a lawsuit too, I haven't heard, but I bet that a lot of people who knew this woman and have experienced her tantrums in the past probably had to snicker to themselves. I guess the reason this came to mind is because I bet that some of the people who knew Jezabel probably snickered to themselves as well.

P.S.—I certainly love and respect my elders, and my juniors, but I don't respect pride and arrogance at any age.

There's lots more to the story if you look in 1 Kings

P.P.S.—The lady who got tazed appeared on the Today show. An official in Texas said that it was a miscarriage of justice, or something like that, but that she has already received

$40,000 from a lawsuit for her pain and humiliation. The woman even admitted on the Today show that she was rude and out of control, that she has those fits a couple of times a year. My underlying snicker remains.

"The Death of Jezebel" by Gustav Doré.
Jezebel was a treacherous woman, and as often happens, those who live by the sword, die by the sword. The dogs in the picture are ready to eat Jezebel, all but her hands.
(Courtesy Wikipedia/Wikimedia)[14]

There's lots more to the story if you look in 1 Kings

The Ol' Turkey Hunter

Tale #4
The Witch of Endor

as told by

"The Ol' Turkey Hunter"

I've tried to have a picture that is somewhat connected to the theme of the chapter, so you know what this picture should be about. Of course, the obvious picture for me would be my mother-in-law, but that would get me in big trouble. Actually, my wife's parents are the best in-laws anyone could ever ask for. My wife has even commented that they like me better than they like her. I don't know about that, but my mother-in-law does fix me a separate little pot of baked beans and potato salad without onions. I'm pretty spoiled. And her coconut cream pie or custard pie, MMMMMMMMMM!!!!!!!!!!!!!!!!!

Back to the picture, I'm sure you have a picture in your mind that will fit in the box very nicely.

The Ol' Turkey Hunter

.

The Witch of Endor

I enjoy physics, or the physical laws of nature. There is energy all around us. One kind of energy that is very intriguing is light energy. So let's look at how light works. Maybe from general science class when you were a freshman, you remember about Roy G. Biv. R-red; o-orange; y-yellow; G.-green; B-blue; i-indigo; and v-violet; the primary colors. The white light we see consists of electromagnetic waves of various lengths. Here is some info from NASA, the National Aeronautics and Space Administration. Sorry it's not in color. Costs too much for me to publish a color book, but you can look it up on the internet. It's very interesting.

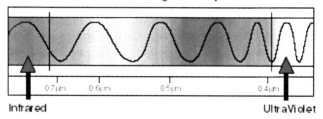

Visible light
Picture courtesy NASA[15]

"On it's Web site, NASA states that Visible light waves are the only electromagnetic waves we can see. We see these waves as the colors of the rainbow. Each color has a different wavelength. Red has the longest wavelength and violet has the shortest wavelength. When all the waves are seen together, they make white light. when white light shines through a prism, the white light is broken apart into the colors of the visible light spectrum. Water vapor in the atmosphere can also break apart wavelengths creating a rainbow.

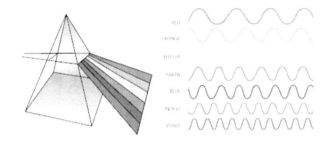

Prism and wavelength
Pictures courtesy NASA[16]

"Each color in a rainbow corresponds to a different wavelength of the electromagnetic spectrum.

The thing that intrigues me is that narrow band of electromagnetic waves right between red and infrared. The orange waves are just as close to the red wavelengths as the infrared waves are, but we can see the orange color and not the infrared. Why is that? But the infrared waves are still there. We know the infrared waves are there because we can feel the heat like that of an infrared heater, we just can't see the color. Or maybe we can. Night vision goggles and night vision photography would not be possible without infrared waves. So I guess we can see infrared light but only under certain conditions.

I go through this science lesson to open your mind to the next Bizarre Short Story from the Bible. It involves Israel's first king, King Saul, and the Witch of Endor.

Now it came about in those days that the Philistines gathered their armed camps for war, to fight against Israel. And Achish [*leader of the Philistines*] said to David [*future King of Israel. At this point in time King Saul was trying to kill David, mostly out of jealousy and Saul knew that David was anointed to rule Israel as successor to his throne*], "Know assuredly that you will go out with me in the camp, you and your men." David said to Achish, "Very well, you shall know what your servant can do." So Achish said to David, "Very well, I will make you my bodyguard for life."

Even in the old days, it seems that politics makes for strange bed fellows. The future king of Israel teaming up with the mortal enemies of Israel in a battle royale.

Now Samuel was dead, and all Israel had lamented him and buried him in Ramah, his own city. And Saul had removed from the land those who were mediums and spiritists.

So the Philistines gathered together and came and camped in Shunem; and Saul gathered all Israel together and they camped in Gilboa. When Saul saw the camp of the Philistines, he was afraid and his heart trembled greatly. When Saul inquired of the LORD, the LORD did not answer him, either by dreams or by Urim or by prophets. Then Saul said to his servants, "Seek for me a woman who is a medium, that I may go to her and inquire of her." And his servants said to him, "Behold, there is a woman who is a medium at Endor."

Then Saul disguised himself by putting on other clothes, and went, he and two men with him, and they came to the woman by night; and he said, "Conjure up for me, please, and bring up for me whom I shall name to you." But the woman said to him, "Behold, you know what Saul has done, how he has cut off those who are mediums and spiritists from the land. Why are you then laying a snare for my life to bring about my death?"

Saul vowed to her by the LORD, saying, "As the LORD lives, no punishment shall come upon you for this thing." Then the woman said, "Whom shall I bring up for you?" And he said, "Bring up Samuel for me."

Saul and witch
Benjamin West, 1777
(Courtesy Wikipedia/Wikimedia)[17]

When the woman saw Samuel, she cried out with a loud voice; and the woman spoke to Saul, saying, "Why have you deceived me? For you are Saul." The king said to her, "Do not be afraid; but what do you see?" And the woman said to Saul, "I see a divine being coming up out of the earth." He said to her, "What is his form?" And she said, "An old man is coming up, and he is wrapped with a robe." And Saul knew that it was Samuel, and he bowed with his face to the ground and did homage.

Apparition of the spirit of Samuel to Saul, by Salvator Rosa, 1668.
(Courtesy Wikipedia/Wikimedia)[18]

Then Samuel said to Saul, "Why have you disturbed me by bringing me up?" And Saul answered, "I am greatly distressed; for the Philistines are waging war against me, and God has departed from me and no longer answers me, either through prophets or by dreams; therefore I have called you, that you may make known to me what I should do."

Samuel said, "Why then do you ask me, since the LORD has departed from you and has become your adversary? The LORD has done accordingly as He spoke through me; for the LORD has torn the kingdom out of your hand and given it to your neighbor, to David. As you did not obey the LORD and did not execute His fierce wrath on Amalek, so the LORD has done this thing to you this day. Moreover the LORD will also give over Israel along with you into the hands of the Philistines, therefore tomorrow you and your sons will be with me. Indeed the LORD will give over the army of Israel into the hands of the Philistines!"

Then Saul immediately fell full length upon the ground and was very afraid because of the words of Samuel; also there was no strength in him, for he had eaten no food all day and all night. The woman came to Saul and saw that he was terrified, and said to him, "Behold, your maidservant has obeyed you, and I have taken my life in my hand and have listened to your words which you spoke to me. So now also, please listen to the voice of your maidservant, and let me set a piece of bread before you that you may eat and have strength when you go on your way." But he refused and said, "I will not eat." However, his servants together with the woman urged him, and he listened to them So he arose from the ground and sat on the bed. The woman had a fattened calf in the house, and she quickly slaughtered it; and she took flour, kneaded it and baked unleavened bread from it. She brought it before Saul and his servants, and they ate. Then they arose and went away that night.

WHEW!!!!! There's a lot of things to consider after that. Well, first you probably wonder what happened to King Saul. You can read all about that in 1 Samuel 31.

Second, what about that ghost? Was it really Samuel or was it just a vision? Did he come up out of the ground or, like infrared light, was he there all of the time and Saul just couldn't see him? If Samuel was there all of the time, when he died did his body just quit working and his spirit went on like it did when he was alive? And what was Samuel doing before he was disturbed?????

Thirdly, what a hypocrite. Saul was killing all of the witches and spiritualists in the country and then he goes in the middle of the night, disguised, and uses the services that he has condemned.

Many times people do the same thing. We cast dispersions upon others to draw attention away from our own faults or misdeeds. Saul was trying to appear righteous through his actions of getting rid of all the spiritists in the country, but wouldn't get right within himself. I think we see that a lot in politics. Candidates sling mud on opponents and make unrealistic promises to make themselves look good. And in churches!!!! You know what I mean.

At the risk of losing any credibility that I may have established, I would like to add a personal experience. I'll report and you decide.

Through our church, my wife, Katie, and I became good friends to Jim and Cindy, another couple in their 50's. Cindy reminded me of Fran Drescher, The Nanny on TV. Cindy had a slow, nasally way of talking. I tormented her a lot, and when she couldn't come up with a good response to my harassment, she would just hit me on the shoulder and growl, "Oh, Dave". One of her claims to fame was her fried chicken. It was awesome.

Cindy got cancer and was in pretty bad shape when Preacher Tom, his wife Nancy, my wife Katie and I went to visit her at her home overlooking the Mississippi River. She was in good spirits and glad to see us because she had been confined to her home or the hospital for several weeks.

Cindy was mobile, but on oxygen, so she had to pull 50 feet of that plastic tubing around the house and had the little plastic tubes sticking up her nose. My wife Katie told Cindy about visiting an elderly man on oxygen and Katie was accidentally standing on the tubing which shut off his oxygen. He got a little frantic for a minute. That got a little laugh, so I persisted in my own obnoxious way.

I asked Cindy if those tubes up her nose caused her any problems getting boogers out of her nose. She laughed and said, in that slow, nasally drawl, "Well, Dave, sometimes you just have to take it out and go for it, Ahhhh, Hahhhh, Hahhhh."

We finished up our visit and said our good-byes. Cindy died ten days later.

About six months after Cindy's death, I was working at a large manufacturing company that makes roller bearings which are used in engines and wheels and things that go round and round. I ran a Cincinnati grinder and I ground heat treated steel bearing races (the outside of a bearing) down to dimensions with a tolerance of $\pm.0002$ inch.

One day I was using an electric pallet jack (or mule) to get a tank of raw parts. The mule had a handle that swivels to steer the load and a control on the handle you twist one way to go forward and the opposite way to go backward. I was back in the warehouse by myself getting a tank of raw stock when my nose started itching. I had gloves on, so I took off my right glove and picked-itched my nose.

When I picked my nose, I was just thinking about Cindy and boogers and her oxygen hoses. The voice in my head was saying, in a slow, nasally drawl, "Well, Dave, sometimes you just have to take it out and go for it, Ahhh, Hahhhh, Hah....BANG! Just as I was still smiling and laughing about Cindy in my head, the swivel handle of the mule smacked me in the hip hard enough to hurt a little. Instantly, I knew that she had hit me for making fun of her, just like she used to hit me when I teased her at church.

A poor reenactment of the Turkey Hunter getting hit in the hip with the handle of an electric pallet jack when making fun of Cindy.
Photo by Author

So, did Cindy's spirit have anything to do with that incident, or was it just remarkably coincidental with absolutely perfect timing? I don't know.

Then to make things a little more bizarre, I was turkey hunting last spring. I'd been in the field four days with no success. On the fifth morning, I was following gobblers, but I couldn't catch up with them, so I just went and sat down in a ditch in a harvested cornfield. I couldn't hear a turkey anywhere and it was my last day of season.

As I was sitting there, enjoying the sunshine and warmth of a clear spring morning, I was contemplating the poison ivy plant that I was sitting by and envisioning how the blooms would develop on the blackberry briar that arched across the ditch. Also, I was thinking about red and infrared when a random thought crossed my mind. I thought, "Hey, Cindy, why don't you drive a turkey to me?" Then I laughed to myself and thought, "That's crazy, Cindy couldn't herd a turkey for nothing." Well, about ten minutes later I heard a turkey gobble way off in the distance, so I called back to him. A few minutes later he gobbled again, quite a bit closer. I called softly again and tried to decide where he was going to come out of the brush and got ready to shoot. The turkey gobbled again and I saw him through the brush about 20 yards away, but I couldn't shoot. There were two of them and they looked like twins.

To make a long story short, I got my gobbler at about 40 yards out in the wide open field. He was a very large bird with an eleven inch beard and 1 ½ inch spurs. His feathers were iridescent and changed colors from shiny yellow to shiny green to shiny indigo as the sunlight bounced from them at different angles. Those two turkeys made a beeline to me, just like someone was herding them to me. I couldn't have asked for more.

The Turkey Hunter and the Cindy turkey.
Photo by author.

So then I have to ask myself again, did Cindy's spirit have anything to do with that incident or was it just remarkably coincidental with absolutely perfect timing? I don't know. I'll report, you decide.
To read about the Witch of Endor, look in 1 Samuel 28.

Tale #5
The Handwriting on the Wall

as told by

"The Ol' Turkey Hunter"

Shown here playing cards. Turkey hunters play many different kinds of card games. Competitor Rob, shown below, is an honorary turkey hunter and a patriot. When stationed in Iraq, Rob toured Babylon and visited the place where King Nebuchadnezzar's throne was located. That helps me realize that there really was a King Nubuchadnezzar, it's not just a story.

The Ol' Turkey Hunter

The Handwriting on the Wall

Many times I've heard the phrase, "the handwriting on the wall". I always took that phrase to mean that what was written was final. And I thought that it was the "handwriting" (like printing or cursive) on the wall (like on the wall of a public restroom).

But later, I realized that it could be the "hand" (an appendage) "writing" (a verb) on the wall. Most parents have experienced a child writing on a wall or door. That could be scary for the child when Mom finds the "handwriting" on her pretty wall, but that's nothing compared to the horror of seeing a "human hand" actually "writing" on the wall. Let me explain what I mean.

Moses led the Israelites to the Promised Land. The children of Abraham had agreed to a contract with God that they would not worship the god's of Canaan, but it wasn't long before they were worshiping Baal and Ashtoreth on every high place as well as in the temple. They even sacrificed their own children to their idols, an act which God had never even considered. So God sent prophets like Jeremiah and Isaiah to try to bring the Israelites back into his good graces, but the Israelites ignored the prophets and even tried to kill them.

So God raised up a mighty army from the north. Nebuchadnezzar, king of the Babylonians, marched upon Judah and laid siege to the capital city, Jerusalem. To starve out the people living inside Jerusalem, the siege lasted about 18 months. It was so horrible that mothers even ate their own children, they were so hungry.

When Jerusalem was finally overrun, the Babylonians killed and destroyed almost everything. They burned the king's palace, Solomon's temple, and the gates to the city. Then they tore down the earthen walls that the Israelites had trusted for protection. All the valuables from King Solomon's temple and other treasures were taken back to Babylon, along with a few survivors of the siege, most notable was a young man named Daniel.

After conquering Judah, King Nebuchadnezzar became very proud and took full credit for all of his accomplishments, so God replaced him with King Belshazzar. Now, here is the rest of the story of the "hand" "writing" on the wall.

> Belshazzar the king held a great feast for a thousand of his nobles, and he was drinking wine in the presence of the thousand. When Belshazzar tasted the wine, he gave orders to bring the gold and silver vessels which Nebuchadnezzar his father had taken out of the temple which was in Jerusalem, so that the king and his nobles, his wives and his concubines might drink from them.
> Then they brought the gold vessels that had been taken out of the temple, the house of God which was in Jerusalem; and the king and his nobles, his wives and his concubines drank from them. They drank the wine and praised the gods of gold and silver, of bronze, iron, wood and stone.
> Suddenly the fingers of a man's hand emerged and began writing opposite the lampstand on the plaster of the wall of the king's palace, and the king saw the back of the hand that did the writing. Then the king's face grew pale and his thoughts alarmed him, and his hip joints went slack and his knees began knocking together.
> The king called aloud to bring in the conjurers, the Chaldeans and the diviners The king spoke and said to the wise men of Babylon, "Any man who can read this inscription and explain its interpretation to me shall be clothed with purple and have a necklace of gold around his neck, and have authority as third ruler in the kingdom."

Golden goblets
Since the Turkey Hunter couldn't find a good picture of real golden goblets that weren't copywrited, he staged this picture of glass goblets painted gold to represent the golden goblets from King Solomon's Temple.
Photo by author.

Then all the king's wise men came in, but they could not read the inscription or make known its interpretation to the king. Then King Belshazzar was greatly alarmed, his face grew even paler, and his nobles were perplexed.

The queen entered the banquet hall because of the words of the king and his nobles; the queen spoke and said, "O king, live forever! Do not let your thoughts alarm you or your face be pale. There is a man in your kingdom in whom is a spirit of the holy gods; and in the days of your father, illumination, insight and

Hand writing on the wall
Rembrandt van Rijn
(1606–1669)

Wikipedia says, "According to Daniel 5:1-31, King Belshazzar of Babylon takes sacred golden and silver vessels from the Jewish Temple in Jerusalem by his predecessor Nebuchadnezzar. Using these holy items, the King and his court praise 'the gods of gold and silver, bronze, iron, wood, and stone'. Immediately, the disembodied fingers of a human hand appear and write on the wall of the royal palace the words "MENE", "MENE", "TEKEL", "PARSIN" (or "UPHARSIN" in a slightly different interpretation of the word)."

(Courtesy Wikipedia/Wikimedia)[19]

wisdom like the wisdom of the gods were found in him And King Nebuchadnezzar, your father, your father the king, appointed him chief of the magicians, conjurers,

Chaldeans and diviners. "This was because an extraordinary spirit, knowledge and insight, interpretation of dreams, explanation of enigmas and solving of difficult problems were found in this Daniel, whom the king named Belteshazzar. Let Daniel now be summoned and he will declare the interpretation."

Then Daniel was brought in before the king. The king spoke and said to Daniel, "Are you that Daniel who is one of the exiles from Judah, whom my father the king brought from Judah? Now I have heard about you that a spirit of the gods is in you, and that illumination, insight and extraordinary wisdom have been found in you. Just now the wise men and the conjurers were brought in before me that they might read this inscription and make its interpretation known to me, but they could not declare the interpretation of the message. But I personally have heard about you, that you are able to give interpretations and solve difficult problems. Now if you are able to read the inscription and make its interpretation known to me, you will be clothed with purple and wear a necklace of gold around your neck, and you will have authority as the third ruler in the kingdom."

Then Daniel answered and said before the king, "Keep your gifts for yourself or give your rewards to someone else; however, I will read the inscription to the king and make the interpretation known to him.

"O king, the Most High God granted sovereignty, grandeur, glory and majesty to Nebuchadnezzar your father. Because of the grandeur which He bestowed on him, all the peoples, nations and men of every language_feared and trembled before him; whomever he wished he killed and whomever he wished he spared alive; and whomever he wished he elevated and whomever he wished he humbled. But when his heart was lifted up and his spirit became so proud that he behaved arrogantly, he was deposed from his royal throne and his glory was taken away from him.

He was also driven away from mankind, and his heart was made like that of beasts, and his dwelling place was with the wild donkeys He was given grass to eat like cattle, and his body was drenched with the dew of heaven until he recognized that the Most High God is ruler over the realm of mankind and that He sets over it whomever He wishes.

"Yet you, his son, Belshazzar, have not humbled your heart, even though you knew all this, but you have exalted yourself against the Lord of heaven; and they have brought the vessels of His house before you, and you and your nobles, your wives and your concubines have been drinking wine from them; and you have praised the gods of silver and gold, of bronze, iron, wood and stone, which do not see, hear or understand. But the God in whose hand are your life-breath and all your ways, you have not glorified. Then the hand was sent from Him and this inscription was written out.

Picture of balance scales
Author L.Miguel Bugallo Sánchez
(Courtesy Wikipedia/Wikimedia)[20]

"Now this is the inscription that was written out: 'MENE, MENE, TEKEL, UPHARSIN.' This is the interpretation of the message: 'MENE'--God has numbered your kingdom and put an end to it. 'TEKEL'--you have been weighed on the scales and found deficient. 'PERES'--your kingdom has been divided and given over to the Medes and Persians."

Then Belshazzar gave orders, and they clothed Daniel with purple and put a necklace of gold around his neck, and issued a proclamation concerning him that he now had authority as the third ruler in the kingdom. That same night Belshazzar the Chaldean king was slain.

So now, when someone says something about "the hand writing on the wall", I know that it's over. And obviously history repeats itself. I see Enron, Bernie Madhoff, some of the big financial institutions, I'm sure they all saw "the hand writing on the wall". So many examples where "pride goeth before a fall". The lesson here is obvious.

This original story is found in and around Daniel 5.

The Ol' Turkey Hunter

Tale #6

Empires Rise and Fall

as told by

"The Ol' Turkey Hunter"

Shown here with a half bushel of hickory nuts. Big L, our beagle pup, is at the stage where he wants to chew on anything. Maybe he is some relation to a squirrel?

The Ol' Turkey Hunter

Empires Rise and Fall

"What goes up must come down". I've heard that lots of times. And "pride goeth before a fall". I love the old sayings that my grandparents and their friends used to quote. There is a lot of truth and common sense in some of the old sayings. And when you learn the origins of the wise sayings, they make sense.

Like "He got my goat." Race horses are highly spirited animals and tightly wound. They have so much energy that they need a calming influence, but unlike humans, they can't live on Valium all the time. So many horse trainers would keep a goat to befriend their race horse and help settle the restless horse's nerves.

As you would expect, people are ruthless and some "cheaters" learned that it would upset the racehorse if his companion, the goat, went missing, so before a big race, a challenger might make arrangements to steal the competitions goat and thus disrupt the horse's schedule causing him to race poorly. So is the origin of "He got my goat".

How did we get to talking about goats? I wanted to talk about the fall of the Egyptian Empire. I once heard it explained about the Roman Empire, maybe not what caused the collapse, but a symptom or characteristic of it. It seems that empires start out with a mission or a hunger, some specific goal in mind, but as these goals are accomplished, all of the dynamics seem to change.

This particular evaluation addresses how the Romans treated their poor people. In the beginning, I'm sure that family and church took care of their own, but then government stepped in, kind of like the U.S. today. The government of Rome, like our politicians today, wants to justify its existence, so they initiated a program to give wheat to the poor. At first, the people are extremely grateful for the assistance. But over time, that isn't enough. So then the government starts handing out flour to those in need. This gave some people work, but to all those receiving assistance, it took away the chore of grinding the wheat into flour which they really needed to do for themselves to occupy some of their time and give them some self worth. But then to look good and stay in power, the rulers decided flour wasn't good enough, so they started to bake the bread and give bread to the people who wanted assistance. And then, if he gets it, I should get it, and on, and on, and on. And it seems to me that one extreme follows another.

Another extreme is in the weather. In the 80's, western Illinois experienced extreme drought and Hancock County was declared a disaster area four different years due to these extremely dry periods. Then the 90's brought some extreme rainfall and flooding of the Mississippi River. You've probably seen the pictures of houses being washed away when the levies were breeched and the water rushed to fill the bottom land along the river. A neighbor that we farmed with when I was young, old Chris Post, always said, "All signs fail in flood and drought". When things are normal, you can expect the weather to react predictably, but in abnormal weather patterns, all bets are off.

That reminds me of the Indian Chief that wanted to maintain his status with the tribe as they moved into the modern era. Anyway, the Indians came to the chief and wanted to know what kind of winter was coming and how they should prepare the camp. The chief said he would go into the wilds, observe nature, and report back to them based upon what he had learned about weather sign from his ancestors.

So the chief went out into the wilderness and observed nature. He looked at the bark on the trees, and the green stuff that grew on the north side of the trees. He checked the thickness of the hulls on the walnuts. He watched the fish in the little streams and which way they swam. He shot a squirrel with his bow and arrow and examined the pelt of the squirrel for thickness and texture. He listened to the wind for ancient signs about the coming winter.

After all of this, he didn't have a clue about what to expect, so he played it safe and told the tribesmen that it was going to be an average winter, and that they should cut some wood. So they did.

A few days later, when the chief was in town, he saw the local meteorologist. Chief asked him for his prediction, and the meteorologist hedged a little and said maybe it might be a little cooler than normal, so the chief went back home and told the braves that new signs told him maybe the winter would be a little cooler than normal, so they need to cut a little more wood. So they did.

A week later, chief ran into the meteorologist again, so he asked if his prediction still stood. "Well, indications are that this could be a really cold winter." So the chief went back to camp and said, "More wood". So they did.

The next week in town, when the meteorologist saw the chief, he came running and waving his arms. "Chief, Chief, it looks like we are going to have one of the worst winters ever. We're looking for snow and ice and wind chills, it could be one of the worst ever."

The chief rubbed his chin and skeptically asked what the meteorologist based this forecast on. The meteorologist said, "The Indians are cutting wood like crazy!"

I think that I was talking about extremes following extremes when I got sidetracked. Poverty following plenty. When I walk into a Wal-Mart SuperCenter it almost scares me the amount and variety of food. We are so blessed to live in this place and time in history, I don't think we appreciate it.

An 'ole boy in my Sunday School class once said that we have it better than kings did in ancient times. WOW! Think about it. The poor people in America have it better than the kings of old. In many, many ways that is true. A Dairy Queen hot fudge sundae. Fresh food from all over the world. Bananas are Wal-Mart's #1 selling item. King crab from Alaska. Lobster. Coffee. Oranges any time of year. Air conditioning. Insect repellant. Dancing girls, just turn on the TV. Naked dancing girls, go to the video store. Live naked dancing girls, you don't have to go to Vegas. Conveniences and excesses of every sort.

P.S. When my wife proof read this chapter, her only comment was, "I don't know where the dancing girls come from?" At first, I was going to say that only the nobility had dancing girls back in the day, but then I thought, "Hummm!!" Well, I'd better leave it at that.

But on the other hand, in another Bible story it talks about plenty after poverty.

> Now it came about after this, that Ben-hadad king of Aram gathered all his army and went up and besieged Samaria.
> There was a great famine in Samaria; and behold, they besieged it, until a donkey's head was sold for eighty shekels of silver, and a fourth of a kab of dove's dung for five shekels of silver.

As the king of Israel was passing by on the wall a woman cried out to him, saying, "Help, my lord, O king!"

He said, "If the LORD does not help you, from where shall I help you? From the threshing floor, or from the wine press?"

And the king said to her, "What is the matter with you?" And she answered, "This woman said to me, 'Give your son that we may eat him today, and we will eat my son tomorrow.'

"So we boiled my son and ate him; and I said to her on the next day, 'Give your son, that we may eat him'; but she has hidden her son."

When the king heard the words of the woman, he tore his clothes--now he was passing by on the wall-- and the people looked, and behold, he had sackcloth beneath on his body. **(Sackcloth was scratchy and worn at times of mourning.)**

Then he said, "May God do so to me and more also, if the head of Elisha the son of Shaphat remains on him today."

Now Elisha was sitting in his house, and the elders were sitting with him. And the king sent a man from his presence; but before the messenger came to him, he **(Elijah)** said to the elders, "Do you see how this son of a murderer has sent to take away my head? Look, when the messenger comes, shut the door and hold the door shut against him. Is not the sound of his master's feet behind him?"

While he was still talking with them, behold, the messenger came down to him and he said, " Behold, this evil is from the LORD; why should I wait for the LORD any longer?"

Then Elisha said, "Listen to the word of the LORD; thus says the LORD, ' Tomorrow about this time a measure of fine flour will be sold for a shekel, and two measures of barley for a shekel, in the gate of Samaria.'"

Two Shekels

Wikipedia says "Shekel (Hebrew: שקל), also rendered sheqel, refers to one of many ancient units of weight and currency. The first known usage is from Mesopotamia around 3000 BC. One explanation is given for the origination of this word as to have originally applied to a specific mass of barley, and the first syllable of the word, 'she' was Akkadian for barley. A shekel was originally 180 grains (~11 grams)."

(Courtesy Wikipedia/Wikimedia)[21]

The royal officer on whose hand the king was leaning answered the man of God and said, "Behold, if the LORD should make windows in heaven, could this thing be?" Then he **(Elijah)** said, "Behold, you will see it with your own eyes, but you will not eat of it."

Now there were four leprous men at the entrance of the gate; and they said to one another, "Why do we sit here until we die?

"If we say, 'We will enter the city,' then the famine is in the city and we will die there; and if we sit here, we die also. Now therefore come, and let us go over to the camp of the Arameans. If they spare us, we will live; and if they kill us, we will but die."

Man with Leprosy
Wikipedia says "24 years old man from Norway,
suffering from leprosy. Leprosy was a contagious,
disfiguring disease that was feared by rich and poor, and
people afflicted were banished to isolation in the leper
colonies."
(Courtesy Wikipedia/Wikimedia)[22]

They arose at twilight to go to the camp of the
Arameans; when they came to the outskirts of the camp
of the Arameans, behold, there was no one there.

For the Lord had caused the army of the
Arameans to hear a sound of chariots and a sound of
horses, even the sound of a great army, so that they
said to one another, "Behold, the king of Israel has
hired against us the kings of the Hittites and the kings
of the Egyptians, to come upon us."

Therefore they arose and fled in the twilight,
and left their tents and their horses and their donkeys,
even the camp just as it was, and fled for their life.

When these lepers came to the outskirts of the
camp, they entered one tent and ate and drank, and
carried from there silver and gold and clothes, and went
and hid them; and they returned and entered another
tent and carried from there also, and went and hid
them.

Then they said to one another, "We are not doing right. This day is a day of good news, but we are keeping silent; if we wait until morning light, punishment will overtake us. Now therefore come, let us go and tell the king's household."

So they came and called to the gatekeepers of the city, and they told them, saying, "We came to the camp of the Arameans, and behold, there was no one there, nor the voice of man, only the horses tied and the donkeys tied, and the tents just as they were."

The gatekeepers called and told it within the king's household.

Then the king arose in the night and said to his servants, "I will now tell you what the Arameans have done to us. They know that we are hungry; therefore they have gone from the camp to hide themselves in the field, saying, 'When they come out of the city, we will capture them alive and get into the city.'"

One of his servants said, "Please, let some men take five of the horses which remain, which are left in the city. Behold, they will be in any case like all the multitude of Israel who are left in it; behold, they will be in any case like all the multitude of Israel who have already perished, so let us send and see."

They took therefore two chariots with horses, and the king sent after the army of the Arameans, saying, "Go and see."

They went after them to the Jordan, and behold, all the way was full of clothes and equipment which the Arameans had thrown away in their haste. Then the messengers returned and told the king.

So the people went out and plundered the camp of the Arameans. Then a measure of fine flour was sold for a shekel and two measures of barley for a shekel, according to the word of the LORD.

Now the king appointed the royal officer on whose hand he leaned to have charge of the gate; but the people trampled on him at the gate, and he died just as the man of God had said, who spoke when the king came down to him.

It happened just as the man of God had spoken to the king, saying, "Two measures of barley for a shekel and a measure of fine flour for a shekel, will be sold tomorrow about this time at the gate of Samaria."

Then the royal officer answered the man of God and said, "Now behold, if the LORD should make windows in heaven, could such a thing be?" And he said, "Behold, you will see it with your own eyes, but you will not eat of it."

And so it happened to him, for the people trampled on him at the gate and he died.

How does this tie in to the Bizarre story of Joseph? The point I'm trying to make is that one extreme follows another and the story of Joseph is a long way to make that point, there are so many other things involved. Let's take a look.

Now Jacob lived in the land where his father had sojourned, in the land of Canaan. These are the records of the generations of Jacob. Joseph, when seventeen years of age, was pasturing the flock with his brothers while he was still a youth, along with the sons of Bilhah and the sons of Zilpah, his father's wives And Joseph brought back a bad report about them to their father.

Now Israel (that's God's new name for Jacob) loved Joseph more than all his sons, because he was the son of his old age; and he made him a varicolored tunic. His brothers saw that their father loved him more than all his brothers; and so they hated him and could not speak to him on friendly terms.

Maize shocks, or bundles, are a traditional harvest practice.
This may be hard to see in the picture, but the piles of
straw are called sheaves. The wheat is cut with a scythe and
the straw with the grain still in the grain heads is stacked so
the rain will run off the side of the sheaves until the grain is
threshed and separated from the straw. This makes a very
understandable dream when eleven of the piles of straw bow
down to the twelfth pile.
(Courtesy Wikipedia/Wikimedia)[23]

Then Joseph had a dream, and when he told it
to his brothers, they hated him even more. He said to
them, "Please listen to this dream which I have had; for
behold, we were binding sheaves in the field, and lo, my
sheaf rose up and also stood erect; and behold, your
sheaves gathered around and bowed down to my
sheaf."

Then his brothers said to him, "Are you actually
going to reign over us? Or are you really going to rule
over us?" So they hated him even more for his dreams
and for his words.

Now he had still another dream, and related it to his brothers, and said, "Lo, I have had still another dream; and behold, the sun and the moon and eleven stars were bowing down to me. **(Joseph had eleven brothers)**" He related it to his father and to his brothers; and his father rebuked him and said to him, "What is this dream that you have had? Shall I and your mother and your brothers actually come to bow ourselves down before you to the ground?"

His brothers were jealous of him, but his father kept the saying in mind. Then his brothers went to pasture their father's flock in Shechem. Israel said to Joseph, "Are not your brothers pasturing the flock in Shechem? Come, and I will send you to them." And he said to him, "I will go." Then he said to him, "Go now and see about the welfare of your brothers and the welfare of the flock, and bring word back to me." So he sent him from the valley of Hebron, and he came to Shechem.

A man found him, and behold, he was wandering in the field; and the man asked him, "What are you looking for?" He said, "I am looking for my brothers; please tell me where they are pasturing the flock." Then the man said, "They have moved from here; for I heard them say, 'Let us go to Dothan.'" So Joseph went after his brothers and found them at Dothan.

When they saw him from a distance and before he came close to them, they plotted against him to put him to death. They said to one another, "Here comes this dreamer!" Now then, come and let us kill him and throw him into one of the pits; and we will say, 'A wild beast devoured him.' Then let us see what will become of his dreams!"

But Reuben heard this and rescued him out of their hands and said, "Let us not take his life." Reuben further said to them, "Shed no blood. Throw him into this pit that is in the wilderness, but do not lay hands on him"--that he might rescue him out of their hands, to restore him to his father.

So it came about, when Joseph reached his brothers, that they stripped Joseph of his tunic, the varicolored tunic that was on him; and they took him and threw him into the pit. Now the pit was empty, without any water in it.

Then they sat down to eat a meal. And as they raised their eyes and looked, behold, a caravan of Ishmaelites was coming from Gilead, with their camels bearing aromatic gum and balm and myrrh, on their way to bring them down to Egypt. Judah said to his brothers, "What profit is it for us to kill our brother and cover up his blood?

"Come and let us sell him to the Ishmaelites and not lay our hands on him, for he is our brother, our own flesh." And his brothers listened to him. Then some Midianite traders passed by, so they pulled him up and lifted Joseph out of the pit, and sold him to the Ishmaelites for twenty shekels of silver Thus they brought Joseph into Egypt.

Now Reuben returned to the pit, and behold, Joseph was not in the pit; so he tore his garments. He returned to his brothers and said, "The boy is not there; as for me, where am I to go?" So they took Joseph's tunic, and slaughtered a male goat and dipped the tunic in the blood; and they sent the varicolored tunic and brought it to their father and said, "We found this; please examine it to see whether it is your son's tunic or not."

Then he examined it and said, "It is my son's tunic. A wild beast has devoured him; Joseph has surely been torn to pieces!" So Jacob tore his clothes, and put sackcloth on his loins and mourned for his son many days. Then all his sons and all his daughters arose to comfort him, but he refused to be comforted. And he said, "Surely I will go down to Sheol in mourning for my son." So his father wept for him. Meanwhile, the

Midianites sold him in Egypt to Potiphar, Pharaoh's officer, the captain of the bodyguard.

So Joseph's brothers sold him into slavery into Egypt. Joseph prospered in Egypt until his boss's wife created a big scandal. You can read about that in Genesis about 38 or 39. This landed him in prison where he met two of the pharaoh's staff members.

Then it came about after these things, the cupbearer and the baker for the king of Egypt offended their lord, the king of Egypt. Pharaoh was furious with his two officials, the chief cupbearer and the chief baker. So he put them in confinement in the house of the captain of the bodyguard, in the jail, the same place where Joseph was imprisoned.

The captain of the bodyguard put Joseph in charge of them, and he took care of them; and they were in confinement for some time. Then the cupbearer and the baker for the king of Egypt, who were confined in jail, both had a dream the same night, each man with his own dream and each dream with its own interpretation. When Joseph came to them in the morning and observed them, behold, they were dejected. He asked Pharaoh's officials who were with him in confinement in his master's house, "Why are your faces so sad today?"

Then they said to him, "We have had a dream and there is no one to interpret it." Then Joseph said to them, "Do not interpretations belong to God? Tell it to me, please." So the chief cupbearer told his dream to Joseph, and said to him, "In my dream, behold, there was a vine in front of me; and on the vine were three branches. And as it was budding, its blossoms came out, and its clusters produced ripe grapes. "Now Pharaoh's cup was in my hand; so I took the grapes and squeezed them into Pharaoh's cup, and I put the cup into Pharaoh's hand."

Then Joseph said to him, "This is the interpretation of it: the three branches are three days; within three more days Pharaoh will lift up your head and restore you to your office; and you will put Pharaoh's cup into his hand according to your former custom when you were his cupbearer. "Only keep me in mind when it goes well with you, and please do me a kindness by mentioning me to Pharaoh and get me out of this house. For I was in fact kidnapped from the land of the Hebrews, and even here I have done nothing that they should have put me into the dungeon."

When the chief baker saw that he had interpreted favorably, he said to Joseph, "I also saw in my dream, and behold, there were three baskets of white bread on my head; and in the top basket there were some of all sorts of baked food for Pharaoh, and the birds were eating them out of the basket on my head."

Then Joseph answered and said, "This is its interpretation: the three baskets are three days; within three more days Pharaoh will lift up your head from you and will hang you on a tree, and the birds will eat your flesh off you."

Thus it came about on the third day, which was Pharaoh's birthday, that he made a feast for all his servants; and he lifted up the head of the chief cupbearer and the head of the chief baker among his servants. He restored the chief cupbearer to his office, and he put the cup into Pharaoh's hand; but he hanged the chief baker, just as Joseph had interpreted to them. Yet the chief cupbearer did not remember Joseph, but forgot him.

Now it happened at the end of two full years that Pharaoh had a dream, and behold, he was standing by the Nile. And lo, from the Nile there came up seven cows, sleek and fat; and they grazed in the marsh grass. Then behold, seven other cows came up after them from the Nile, ugly and gaunt, and they stood by the other cows on the bank of the Nile. The ugly and gaunt cows ate up the seven sleek and fat cows. Then Pharaoh awoke.

He fell asleep and dreamed a second time; and behold, seven ears of grain came up on a single stalk, plump and good. Then behold, seven ears, thin and scorched by the east wind, sprouted up after them. The thin ears swallowed up the seven plump and full ears. Then Pharaoh awoke, and behold, it was a dream.

Now in the morning his spirit was troubled, so he sent and called for all the magicians of Egypt, and all its wise men And Pharaoh told them his dreams, but there was no one who could interpret them to Pharaoh.

Then the chief cupbearer spoke to Pharaoh, saying, "I would make mention today of my own offenses. Pharaoh was furious with his servants, and he put me in confinement in the house of the captain of the bodyguard, both me and the chief baker. "We had a dream on the same night, he and I; each of us dreamed according to the interpretation of his own dream." Now a Hebrew youth was with us there, a servant of the captain of the bodyguard, and we related them to him, and he interpreted our dreams for us. To each one he interpreted according to his own dream. "And just as he interpreted for us, so it happened; he restored me in my office, but he hanged him."

Then Pharaoh sent and called for Joseph, and they hurriedly brought him out of the dungeon; and when he had shaved himself and changed his clothes, he came to Pharaoh. Pharaoh said to Joseph, "I have had a dream, but no one can interpret it; and I have heard it said about you, that when you hear a dream you can interpret it."

Joseph then answered Pharaoh, saying, "It is not in me; God will give Pharaoh a favorable answer." So Pharaoh spoke to Joseph, "In my dream, behold, I was standing on the bank of the Nile; and behold, seven cows, fat and sleek came up out of the Nile, and they grazed in the marsh grass.

Joseph interprets the dream of the Pharaoh. Painting by Peter von Cornelius.
(Courtesy Wikipedia/Wikimedia)[24]

Lo, seven other cows came up after them, poor and very ugly and gaunt, such as I had never seen for ugliness in all the land of Egypt; and the lean and ugly cows ate up the first seven fat cows. Yet when they had devoured them, it could not be detected that they had devoured them, for they were just as ugly as before. Then I awoke.

"I saw also in my dream, and behold, seven ears, full and good, came up on a single stalk; and lo, seven ears, withered, thin, and scorched by the east wind, sprouted up after them; and the thin ears swallowed the seven good ears. Then I told it to the magicians, but there was no one who could explain it to me."

Now Joseph said to Pharaoh, "Pharaoh's dreams are one and the same; God has told to Pharaoh what He is about to do. The seven good cows are seven years; and the seven good ears are seven years; the dreams are one and the same. The seven lean and ugly cows that came up after them are seven years, and the seven thin ears scorched by the east wind will be seven years of famine. It is as I have spoken to Pharaoh: God has shown to Pharaoh what He is about to do. Behold, seven years of great abundance are coming in all the land of Egypt; and after them seven years of famine will come, and all the abundance will be forgotten in the land of Egypt, and the famine will ravage the land." So the abundance will be unknown in the land because of that subsequent famine; for it will be very severe. Now as for the repeating of the dream to Pharaoh twice, it means that the matter is determined by God, and God will quickly bring it about. Now let Pharaoh look for a man discerning and wise, and set him over the land of Egypt. Let Pharaoh take action to appoint overseers in charge of the land, and let him exact a fifth of the produce of the land of Egypt in the seven years of abundance. Then let them gather all the food of these good years that are coming, and store up the grain for food in the cities under Pharaoh's authority, and let them guard it. Let the food become as a reserve for the land for the seven years of famine which will occur in the land of Egypt, so that the land will not perish during the famine."

Now the proposal seemed good to Pharaoh and to all his servants. Then Pharaoh said to his servants, "Can we find a man like this, in whom is a divine spirit?" So Pharaoh said to Joseph, "Since God has informed you of all this, there is no one so discerning and wise as you are. You shall be over my house, and according to your command all my people shall do homage; only in the throne I will be greater than you." Pharaoh said to Joseph, "See, I have set you over all the land of Egypt." Then Pharaoh took off his signet ring from his hand and put it on Joseph's hand, and clothed him in garments of fine linen and put the gold necklace around his neck. He had him ride in his second chariot;

and they proclaimed before him, "Bow the knee!" And he set him over all the land of Egypt.

Moreover, Pharaoh said to Joseph, "Though I am Pharaoh, yet without your permission no one shall raise his hand or foot in all the land of Egypt." Then Pharaoh named Joseph Zaphenath-paneah; and he gave him Asenath, the daughter of Potiphera priest of On, as his wife. And Joseph went forth over the land of Egypt. Now Joseph was thirty years old when he stood before Pharaoh, king of Egypt. And Joseph went out from the presence of Pharaoh and went through all the land of Egypt.

During the seven years of plenty the land brought forth abundantly. So he gathered all the food of these seven years which occurred in the land of Egypt and placed the food in the cities; he placed in every city the food from its own surrounding fields. Thus Joseph stored up grain in great abundance like the sand of the sea, until he stopped measuring it, for it was beyond measure.

Now before the year of famine came, two sons were born to Joseph, whom Asenath, the daughter of Potiphera priest of On, bore to him. Joseph named the firstborn Manasseh, "For," he said, "God has made me forget all my trouble and all my father's household." He named the second Ephraim, "For," he said, "God has made me fruitful in the land of my affliction."

When the seven years of plenty which had been in the land of Egypt came to an end, and the seven years of famine began to come, just as Joseph had said, then there was famine in all the lands, but in all the land of Egypt there was bread. So when all the land of Egypt was famished, the people cried out to Pharaoh for bread; and Pharaoh said to all the Egyptians, "Go to Joseph; whatever he says to you, you shall do." When the famine was spread over all the face of the earth, then Joseph opened all the storehouses, and sold to the

Egyptians; and the famine was severe in the land of Egypt. The people of all the earth came to Egypt to buy grain from Joseph, because the famine was severe in all the earth.

So Joseph bought all the land of Egypt for Pharaoh, for every Egyptian sold his field, because the famine was severe upon them. Thus the land became Pharaoh's. As for the people, he removed them to the cities from one end of Egypt's border to the other. Only the land of the priests he did not buy, for the priests had an allotment from Pharaoh, and they lived off the allotment which Pharaoh gave them. Therefore, they did not sell their land.

Then Joseph said to the people, "Behold, I have today bought you and your land for Pharaoh; now, here is seed for you, and you may sow the land. At the harvest you shall give a fifth to Pharaoh, and four-fifths shall be your own for seed of the field and for your food and for those of your households and as food for your little ones." So they said, "You have saved our lives! Let us find favor in the sight of my lord, and we will be Pharaoh's slaves." Joseph made it a statute concerning the land of Egypt valid to this day, that Pharaoh should have the fifth; only the land of the priests did not become Pharaoh's.

This was an example of one extreme following another, extreme plenty following extreme shortage. This happened about the time of the New Kingdom era of Egypt, between the 16th century and 11th century BC, a time that was very prosperous.

Wikipedia says; "The many achievements of the ancient Egyptians include the quarrying, surveying and construction techniques that facilitated the building of monumental pyramids, temples, and obelisks; a system of mathematics, a practical and effective system of medicine, irrigation systems and agricultural production techniques, the first known ships, Egyptian faience and glass technology, new forms of literature, and the earliest known peace treaty. Egypt left a lasting legacy. Its art and architecture were widely copied, and its antiquities

carried off to far corners of the world. Its monumental ruins have inspired the imaginations of travelers and writers for centuries. A newfound respect for antiquities and excavations in the early modern period led to the scientific investigation of
Egyptian civilization and a greater appreciation of its cultural legacy, for Egypt and the world. "

The Egypt of Joseph's day, before the famine, was very prosperous and I believe very proud, as illustrated by the great pyramids and other elaborate burial customs. I can just see the advertisements they would have had back in their day, maybe even a song, "Proud to be an Egyptian".

Fine tin-glazed earthenware (*maiolica*) in traditional pattern, made in Faenza

Wikipedia says "Egyptian faience is a non-clay based ceramic displaying surface vitrification which creates a bright lustre of various colours. Having not been made from clay it is often not classed as pottery. It is called "Egyptian faience" to distinguish it from faience, the tin glazed pottery associated with Faenza in northern Italy. Egyptian faience, both locally produced and exported from Egypt, occurs widely in the ancient world, and is well known from Mesopotamia, the Mediterranean and in northern Europe as far away as Scotland."

Ceramics (Majolica) plate from the Italian city of Faenza decorated with a traditional style. Picture taken on Dec 26, 2005 by Rosco

(Courtesy Wikipedia/Wikimedia)[25]

The Ol' Turkey Hunter

And how quickly things can change. One day they are on top of the world, and a little bit later they are begging for food and selling themselves into slavery just to survive. I worry that "Pride goeth before a fall". One extreme after another. For more information, read the last few chapters of Genesis.

Tale #7
The Maniac of Gadara

as told by

"The Ol' Turkey Hunter"

Shown here with a nice deer. The Turkey Hunter shot this deer to get the pictures to show to the boys at the boys' academy. The teenage boys loved to hear stories and see pictures because they did not have access to TV or radio or internet or phones.

The Ol' Turkey Hunter

The Maniac of Gadara

Like Rodney Dangerfield, pigs get no respect. Most people are turned off by pigs. They stink and they are dirty and ugly and....just yuck!!! But most people are turned on by pork. Bacon, pork chops, ham, BBQ ribs, pulled pork, even pork and beans!!! Bacon goes great with anything, I think it would even go great with cherry pie. There is no part of a pig that isn't good. Pork rinds (that's the fat), everything, you name it, it's good.

Litter of pigs
Modern swine producers do everything possible to maximize productivity, which means the best in nutrition, environment, and health care. This litter of Chester Whites are one of the few breeds that was developed in the United States. They have a combination of meat quality and maternal qualities, large litters and milk production.
Photo courtesy Gerth Hog Farm.[26]

I was raised on a farm and my uncle gave my brother and me 5 runt pigs when I was 8 years old. We kept them in the chicken house.

Then I raised my first litter of purebred Hampshire pigs, black with a white belt around the front legs and shoulders, when I was 10. My brother and I each got a bred gilt, $75 each. I was so excited when the babies came.

Dad had fixed up the old brooder house and put an old section of picket fence between the two mommas and hung heat lights to warm the new babies. I remember getting off the school bus. Dad motioned for us to come out where he was, at the brooder house, so I went running to see what was going on. I still remember the smell of diesel fuel, I don't know why. Maybe Dad had a heater in there that I don't remember. But the mommas were just laying there all stretched out and grunting to their babies, and all of those little black and white piggies. They were like a can of worms. Each was a miniature milking machine. This one would fall over that one until he got his own nipple and ate until one of his brothers would knock him off and then he would root around until he found another dinner plate. And then "BLOOP", there was another baby. He looked like he was dead, but then he would sneeze and shake his head and thrash around, blink his eyes, then he would crawl around mommas back leg, and pretty soon when he dried off, you couldn't tell him from the rest of the babies. I think my brothers gilt had 10 and mine had 13. They were as cute as any animal can be. Since that time I've worked with pigs off and on for 50 years.

Pigs are incredible animals. They seem to be the most like humans of any animal. Pigs have saved the lives of many people. Pig valves are often used in open heart surgery. I asked a friend if she had a craving for corn after her heart valve replacement surgery. I don't think that was very original and I don't think she appreciated it very much. At least I didn't "oink" at her.

And that reminds me of the pig that saved a farmer and his young family. The farmer lived in a nice, big farmhouse on his acreage. One night when the family was asleep, the farmhouse caught fire. The farmer didn't wake up until his pig started squealing and squealing and squealing. Luckily, the squealing woke up the farmer and he got his family out of the burning building. The farmhouse burned to the ground, but the family was safe.

Grand Champion Duroc Boar

Duroc hogs are red pigs that I believe were imported from Europe. The male hog pictured above is an excellent breeding animal shown by Gerth Hog Farm. Durocs are used in cross-breeding programs for their heavy muscling, fast growth rate, and quality of meat. They are known for a large loin eye, the muscle that runs down the top of their back where pork chops and pork loin come from. I think this is where the saying comes from "eating high on the hog". Nothing better than pork chops on the grill with Lowery's Seasoning Salt. MMMMM!!!! Makes my mouth water.

Photo courtesy Gerth Hog Farm[27]

Word of the pig miracle got out and a reporter from the newspaper came out to investigate. The farmer took the reporter out to see the "hero" pig. The pig was limping from a wooden peg he was using for a back leg, so the reporter asked if the pig was handicapped at the time of the fire. The farmer said, "Oh, no. He's a good pig." So the reporter asked, "So, what's the story on the peg leg?" The farmer replied, "Oh, you don't eat a good pig like that all at once!"

But really, what do you do with a pig. When I was going to college, I worked on a big pig farm. The largest litter I saved had 14 baby pigs. The runt of the litter had a white head and shoulders and

Burning House
I've set many fires in my time, and I think that every one of them got a lot bigger than I expected. I even had to call out the local volunteer fire department one time. Not a good thing.
Photo courtesy Jodi Pospeschil,
Managing Editor, The McDonough County Voice[28]

was black on the hams and back legs, a really cute little piglet. The boss would come in to the farrowing house and pick up that runt pig and carry him around. It was his "little man", wearing a white shirt and black pants.

The boss didn't tell me to move the litter, but as the piggies got bigger and I really needed the space in the farrowing house for more babies, I moved the "little man" and his brothers to the nursery. The

boss's wife flagged me down on the hiway to tell me that I needed to be very careful because if anything happened to the "little man" or his brothers, the boss would probably "let me go". Oh, well. I was looking for a job when I started there. And it's kind of ironic that when I went to interview for the job a bird flew over and pooped on the shoulder of the white T-shirt I was wearing. A sign of things to come??????

But nothing happened to any of them and they eventually grew up. The interesting thing is, as much as the boss loved that "little man", this little piggie still went to market. A pig is a pig is a pig.

I used to teach high school agriculture and observed many similarities between the students and pigs. Both kids and pigs can tear up a steel ball. Both humans and pigs prefer to be clean if given the choice. In an open barn, pigs will go to the bathroom in a corner, out of the main living area. I once heard about a man that had to go to the bathroom and he went into a round barn. I think it was a joke, but I forget what happened to him.

Both kids and pigs are omnivores, eating fruits and vegetables as well as meat. The digestive systems are very similar. Cows and sheep have a 4-chamber stomach which allows them to digest roughages like grass and hay. Pigs and kids both have a simple stomach and both like to eat corn on the cob and beans. And both like to eat chicken.

Roasted chicken

I think that the Broasted Chickens at Wal-Mart and Hy-Vee look better than this, but I wouldn't back away from it. There's not much that's not good on a chicken.

(Courtesy Wikipedia/Wikimedia)[29]

105

The Ol' Turkey Hunter

The barn at the home farm where I grew up.

Us kids spent lots of time in this old barn when we were growing up. We had pigs and chores to take care of, but you never knew what you would find there. In the spring and summer, there were lots of sparrow nests to knock down if you could find a long skinny stick to poke at them. And the little boxes formed by the floor joists were perfect places for baby pigeons to grow up. When I got older, I could put a ladder up to the wall and catch the young squabs. I don't remember what I ever did with them. And the old hens that ran loose would nest up in the top and occasionally there would be a litter of kittens that would need to be tamed.

There were holes in the upstairs floor that were above the feed bunk below so you could throw hay down to the cows. One day one of the holes was covered with straw and my brother Bob was walking over to help me and suddenly, he was gone. We were both surprised when he disappeared, but luckily he wasn't hurt when he fell through the hidden hole in the floor.

The only thing we didn't have in this barn was a hay rope to swing on, but we had that in another barn.

Photo by author.

At the home farm when I was a kid, we had a Quonset barn with a basement under it. We kept our pigs in the bottom, and often times an old hen would hatch out a clutch of chicks in the hay mow above. I know pigs like to eat chicken because one nest of newly hatched chicks was close to a hole in the floor and several chicks fell through the hole, one at a time, before my brother, Bob, and I could catch them. A chick would fall and we would scramble down the ladder just in time to see the pigs smacking their lips after eating the chick. Then we'd go back up and another one would fall and the same thing happened. I was so mad at those pigs, but they enjoyed the chicken dinner just as much as I enjoy Kentucky Fried.

Nest of Chicken Eggs

This is what a chicken nest up in the old barn looked like when I found them. Usually a nest that was set would have about 15 eggs with a few eggs sticking out from under the feathers of a feisty, growling old hen setting on them. Those little old hens would flare up their feathers and peck at you to leave them alone. I was always scared of them, but Grandma Kerr would just grab their head and gather the eggs anyway.

(Courtesy Wikipedia/Wikimedia)[30]

Another similarity between kids and pigs, if you co-mingle pigs from different pens, they will fight to establish a pecking order, and the older they are when co-mingled, the more violent the fights. Four junior high schools sent students to the high school where I taught. During school and after school, the students from the different towns would bicker and physically come to blows. Even 15 years after graduation, I observed softball players from the different junior high's going at it.

Buff Orpington Chick
Buff Orpington is the name of a breed of chicken. They are
dual purpose breed that can be used for egg production and meat
which makes them popular with hobbyist and families. They are usually
a buff, brownish color
(Courtesy Wikipedia/Wikimedia)[31]

A broody mother hen and her chicks.
I guarantee if you get too close to this momma hen she will
make a threatening growl and take a chunk of skin out of your hand. I

wish some parents were that protective of their children. (Note two chicks peaking out from under Mom)

Photo courtesy Randy Stevens, Stevens Poultry Farm

www.stevenspoultryfarm.com[32]

And try to push a pig where he isn't sure he wants to go. Both pigs and people squeal if they are crowded or their rights are infringed. Workers often times have to move pigs from one area to another. The pigs resist the change from their daily routine and often squeal just because. And you hear about people on TV, boy, if you even get close to infringing upon their self-conceived "rights", man, they will squeal like a pig.

Two very lean, muscular Hampshire gilts (females).
These pigs are almost too small to be shoats, but I wanted to put the picture in because my first litter of pigs were Hampshires and they are still my favorite. They are still very popular as a sire breed because of their meatiness. I wonder why they have a white belt around their front legs and shoulders?

Picture courtesy Gerth Hog Farm[33]

And when you move pigs, there is always one in every group. Once I moved a group of 113 shoats, pigs about comparable age-wise to teenagers, and there was one that wouldn't go into the new pen. I chased and chased, but he wouldn't go through the gate and into the pen with the others. I was in my early 20's and could throw pretty good, so I usually threw rocks to encourage the pigs to go where I wanted. This particular pig was out in a grass pasture, so there were no rocks to be had, so I grabbed the only thing I had to throw, my slip-joint pliers that I kept in my hip pocket.

I was pretty mad at this point, so I let them fly. The handle of the pliers stuck in between the pig's ribs, about the middle of his body. Then I thought, "Oh, no. I killed him. And I paid $50 for him." Well, after a little more chasing, the pliers jiggled out and the pig went into the pen. The damage turned out to be minimal and that little piggie went to market with the rest of them.

Now, before any PETA people that may be reading this start having a fit, if you are not a vegetarian, I'd like you to work with some pigs for a week before you pass judgement on me for animal cruelty.

And where was PETA when that singer guy beat up Rhiana? I'm not a very large research staff, but I watch a lot of news programs on NBC, CBS, and Fox, and I read some newspapers and magazines and I didn't hear a word out of PETA concerning the beating she took. I guarantee he inflicted more pain and injury on her than I did on that pig.

> I thought about putting a picture
> of Rihanna in this spot, but she was
> beaten badly and the pictures I found
> were really horrific.

Where was PETA?
Photo by author.

I find people to be very interesting. While working at the boys' school, I gained a lot of insight into what factors caused the students to develop the way they did.

I've concluded, right or wrong, that people really are a lot like computers. Humans and computers both start out as very small but complex entities.

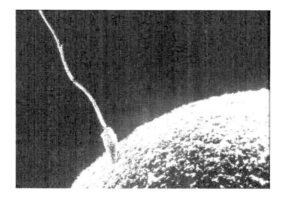

A sperm cell fertilizing an ovum

All people start out this way. This picture is magnified many, many times. It's hard to imagine that "The Refridgerator" Perry, the Chicago Bears football player, started out this small, but he did. How can these two "half-cells" divide into millions of bone cells, muscle cells, brain cells, red blood cells, white blood cells, organs, nerves, hair, fingernails, and skin that all work together to form a functioning human being? There is an amazing set of instructions included within these two little "half-cells".

(Courtesy Wikipedia/Wikimedia)[34]

Microprocessor

This is the mechanical or man made version of a fertilized egg.

It is the part that controls all of the other functions of a computer.

It also has an amazing set of instructions included within itself.

(Courtesy Wikipedia/Wikimedia)[35]

When I was younger, I pondered the question which was more important, heredity or environment. When I was younger, I always thought that heredity was a little more important than environment, but I've mostly changed my mind.

The microprocessor limits the maximum capabilities of a computer, in a perfect world. And heredity limits the maximum capabilities of a human, in a perfect world, but as you know, we don't live in a perfect world.

The actual capabilities of a computer are controlled by all of the factors that it is exposed to, just like people are.

If you add a spreadsheet program to a computer, it will add and subtract and multiply and divide and organize and print and…and…and. If you add a word processor, you can create documents and edit and print them. You can add games and e-mail and news and music and weather and maps and…and…and. This is all good, but no matter how good these things are, if you introduce a virus or cookies or whatever else is out there, your computer can get really sick and may even die. We go to great lengths to put virus protection and fire walls and stuff into place to protect the health of our computer systems.

With a child, the maximum potential is in place at the time of conception. From there, I think that it is mostly downhill. Many things can happen to a child to lower his or her potential, but wait. That can happen even before birth.

The mother has a lot of control over an unborn child through her daily habits. For example, fetal alcohol syndrome can severely restrict the potential of a child. It is widely accepted that excessive alcohol has a detrimental effect upon the brain of adults. So what does it do to a rapidly developing fetus?

And as a newborn child grows and develops, we start to load the programs into the little individual. Love, caring, respect, perseverance, correction, consequences, joy, peace; great programs to load into a child.

And then come the virus. Parents too busy to spend time with the kids, divorce, no structure, permissiveness, drugs, TV and movies, commercials. People are in many ways just like computers. When they say "garbage in, garbage out", I believe it.

So when I consider people who are radically against the abuse of animals, I wonder what programs have been loaded into them.

I am 100% against the cruelty of animals, but apparently my idea of cruelty and others idea of cruelty are quite different.

I say this because of news reports that PETA even criticized the president for swatting a fly that landed on his arm during a TV interview. I have to wonder if these people have ever sat outside on a nice summers evening when a mosquito starts sucking blood out of their arm. As a reaction to the pain of the bite do they politely say, "If you don't get enough blood out of that hole, I think that you will have better luck if you bite over here. Oh, and I'm really looking forward to the totally natural experience of malaria or West Nile Virus that you may be injecting into my bloodstream as we speak."

Or if a deer tick would happen to dig it's mouth parts inextractably through your skin and attach to your side. When the itch starts…., I'm not even going there. My wife can thank a deer tick for the Lyme disease she contracted several years ago which probably led to the rheumatoid arthritis she now has.

I don't know any PETA members, but I'm guessing that their homes or apartments are not overrun with ants, roaches, mice, etc. Why not? Do you suppose that they have an exterminator do the dirty work for them? Just like we all pay to have other people do the dirty work of butchering so we can have the high quality foods we enjoy today.

So if you are not a total vegetarian; and if you have a pair of shoes or boots with leather uppers or leather soles, or leather gloves or leather pants, or leather seats in your automobile, and you belong to PETA,,,,,,,,,,,,

Oh, I was talking about the observation that there is always one in every group. That made me think of the military. I was never in the service, but I suspect that there was some basis for the Gomer Pyle Show. I bet there were times when Sgt. Carter wanted to throw rocks at Gomer Pyle too.

So this is a really big lead up to the first bizarre story in the New Testament. It involves Jesus and a crazy man. Let's see what happens.

Then they sailed to the country of the Gerasenes, which is opposite Galilee. And when He (**Jesus**) came out onto the land, He was met by a man from the city who was possessed with demons; and who had not put on any clothing for a long time, and was not living in a house, but in the tombs.

Seeing Jesus, he cried out and fell before Him, and said in a loud voice, "What business do we have with each other, Jesus, Son of the Most High God? I beg You, do not torment me." For He had commanded the unclean spirit to come out of the man. For it had seized him many times; and he was bound with chains and shackles and kept under guard, and yet he would break his bonds and be driven by the demon into the desert.

And Jesus asked him, "What is your name?" And he said, "Legion"; for many demons had entered him. They were imploring Him not to command them to go away into the abyss. Now there was a herd of many swine feeding there on the mountain; and the demons implored Him to permit them to enter the swine. And He gave them permission.

I'm pretty certain that the swine herders were not Jewish. Up until the time of Jesus, Jews were not allowed to eat pork. It was just one of God's laws. I think the reason Jews considered pork to be unclean was the fact that there were some health risks associated with eating pork. Health experts always tell us to cook pork thoroughly. This is because before modern swine production practices were implemented, pigs would get a parasite called trichina. Thorough cooking would kill this parasite, but if ingested alive, the parasite could cause major health problems in its' human host. Also, pigs used to have 1" to 3" of back fat. Obviously, we now know that eating lots of fat and not exercising can cause us to have problems with cholesterol and obesity. But today, through intelligent design, livestock breeders have developed bloodlines of pigs that have as little as .2" of backfat, which I think makes pork much tastier and healthier.

An extra note, Peter learned through a vision that the old covenant was replaced at Jesus's crucifiction and we are no longer restricted on what foods we can eat, so we eat pork.

> And the demons came out of the man and entered the swine; and the herd rushed down the steep bank into the lake and was drowned. When the herdsmen saw what had happened, they ran away and reported it in the city and out in the country. The people went out to see what had happened; and they came to Jesus, and found the man from whom the demons had gone out, sitting down at the feet of Jesus, clothed and in his right mind; and they became frightened. Those who had seen it reported to them how the man who was demon-possessed had been made well.
>
> And all the people of the country of the Gerasenes and the surrounding district asked Him to leave them, for they were gripped with great fear; and He got into a boat and returned. But the man from whom the demons had gone out was begging Him that he might accompany Him; but He sent him away, saying, "Return to your house and describe what great things God has done for you." So he went away, proclaiming throughout the whole city what great things Jesus had done for him.

Back in the day, they didn't have TV or radio or cell phones or newspapers, so the people lived in relative ignorance compared to today. They didn't hear about shocking news like the tsunami's or 911 attacks or great earthquakes; and they didn't have special effects in the movies. Comparatively, there was little day to day change, and when this astonishing, unexplainable event occurred in their town, the people marveled, but also they were afraid.

To read more about this amazing event, look in Matthew 8, Mark 5, and Luke 8.

The Ol' Turkey Hunter

Tale #8
A Bizarre Short Story
NOT Found
in the Bible

as told by
"The Ol' Turkey Hunter"

Shown below is Old Bill and a bunch of mushrooms (morels).
Turkey hunters also know where all of the mushrooms
grow. He may pick 100 pounds of morels a year and greatly
enjoys giving them away. Despite being wounded in
Vietnam, Bill enjoys the great outdoors; his dogs and
cattle, deer, pheasants, turkeys, rabbits, berries,
mushrooms, and arrow heads; and unfortunately, the Red
Sox.

The Ol' Turkey Hunter

A Bizarre Short Story
NOT Found
in the Bible

I know that this book is about bizarre short stories in the Bible, but this is a pretty bizarre story that I experienced and it may have some relevance to the Bible. So again, at the risk of destroying any credibility I may have established, I'll report and you decide.

Southeastern High School (2008-   )
Augusta, Illinois
Photo by Author

The Ol' Turkey Hunter

I think I've mentioned that I spent two years working with troubled teens at a specialty boarding school in Iowa. It was an awesome situation where I got to experience the application or misapplication of many biblical principles in the everyday life of troubled teens who were basically being held captive, isolated from the negative friends and negative external forces that have caused their parents many sleepless nights. Many times the boys, at the request of their parents, were kidnapped when two big ugly guys would enter their bedroom about 3:00 am, bind their hands with cable ties or handcuffs, and haul them off to Keokuk, Iowa, where they got to spend the next few months or years with us, depending upon how strong-willed they were or how smart they were at learning how to manipulate the system.

The program at the school was **very** strict and structured. Students could not stand up, sit down, talk, anything, without first obtaining permission from a dorm parent. They got up the same time every day and went to bed the same time, and did home schooling at their own pace on the computers in the classrooms at defined times, everything was on a schedule. Level 1's wore plaid ties and received a maintainance diet. Fat kids lost weight and skinny kids bulked up. Level 2's got salad bar in addition to the basic meals. Level 3's got to wear a solid blue tie with their white shirt and blue dress pants. Upper levels wore a solid red tie. Upper level students had earned more freedoms and were not constantly scrutinized by staff like lower levels. Lower level students were watched 24-7-60-60. Twenty four hours, seven days a week, 60 minutes per hour and 60 seconds per minute. No TV, no radio, no computer except for Switched-on Schoolhouse which was the home schooling curriculum. No phone, no texting, no internet. One letter home per week. Incoming mail, twice a week if they received any, was screened closely.

And the dorm parents weren't very average. I'm 5' 10", 225#, and I was a shrimp. Mostly young guys in their 20's and 30's, many of the dorm parents were huge. 6' 5" or more and 285# or more. They were intimidating. Staff members alternated spending the night on call and slept on mattresses in front of any door that was not locked, although all doors were alarmed to discourage students from trying to climb the walls in the middle of the night. One Thanksgiving morning, a "normal size" staff member slept in on his mattress on the floor in front of a door and didn't get up to attend the morning meeting. So after the meeting, four of the other staff members went out to "wake him up". They decided to play "dogpile on Jeremy". 285#, 300#, 275#, and 290#. They piled over 1000# on top of Jeremy on a thin mattress on the cement floor in about 1 ½ seconds. And you know what Jeremy said, "UUUUUUOOOOOOOOHHHHHHHHMMMMMMMMM AAAAAAAAAAAHHHHHHHHHEEEEEEEEEEE!!!!!!!!!!!!!" He never slept in late again.

They say that the definition of insanity is expecting a different result with the same inputs, like putting the kids who had completed the program back in the same situation they had just left and expecting them to behave better.

That reminds me of the two guys that went to a Western movie one night. In the movie, two cowboys were riding their horses as fast as they would go. As the music became more intense, the one moviegoer said, "I bet the bad guy hits that limb and gets knocked off his horse." His buddy said, "I'll take that bet. I bet that he ducks under it."

Sure enough, the cowboy rode into the limb and got knocked off the horse. The buddy that bet the cowboy would duck under the limb said, "Boy, he's not very smart. He got knocked off his horse this afternoon when I watched it and he just let it knock him off again. He didn't learn a thing."

So the boys' academy program, besides providing extreme structure, offers a series of seminars for both the students and the parents. Also, when the boys graduated they often went to live at a different physical location so they did not go back into the same environment that got them into trouble in the first place. Putting the students back in the same home with the same parents and the same environment that produced the problems in the first place without changing the parenting skills and other negative influences would be of no benefit, "insanity".

The school was private and not religiously based, but it used many biblical principles in healing the broken young lives. James 5:16 says, *"Confess your faults one to another, and pray one for another, that ye may be healed."* Guilt was a central problem of the students and guilt was a major cause of low self-esteem. Guilt is a very powerful negative force in all people and it seems that there is an endless supply of sources for guilt.

As it says in James, confession and prayer promotes healing. I've found that forgiveness of self, as well as others, is the cure for guilt. We used two main methods to confess our faults and start the healing process with the student at the school.

One method was "group". Each day, one hour of "group" was scheduled. During "group", a different student would stand up in front of a "family" of 20-25 peers and discuss their problems. I loved group because the students would "bare their souls" to me and the rest of their peers. It seemed that God gave me insights to ask leading questions and a non-judgmental attitude that allowed many guilt issues to come out. It was my intention to have someone crying every day, and it usually happened. Guilt is such a devastating emotion.

One student would tell about what a terrible thing he had done, drugs, girlfriend, date rape, stealing, lying, stabbing, getting shot at, bullying, being bullied, etc. I would then ask what they could do to change what had happened. Each young man knew that there was nothing that could be done to change the past, what was done was done.

Then we would go around the room and ask each family member if they could forgive the one standing and confessing. Everyone could always forgive the offender of his offenses. Everyone, that is, except the person speaking. It's sometimes easy to forgive someone else, but it's really hard to forgive yourself.

After the student had made a confession, standing there alone in front of all of his friends with his head down, looking at the floor in shame, I would often ask if they knew the Lord's Prayer, *"forgive us our trespasses as we forgive those who trespass against us"*. When they said yes, I would ask, "So are you better than God? If you ask God for forgiveness and He forgives you, how can you not forgive yourself?" It was a slow process, but broken bones heal slowly and so do broken hearts and spirits.

The second method we used to confess our faults was the confession letter. Each student was expected to write a confession letter to his parents. They always shared the letter with me. Some confession letters were short, a few pages, and some were up to 40 pages in length. It took a long time to get one of my very favorite kids to write his confession letter (I know you can't have favorites, but I really loved this kid). When he did finally write his letter, he used the very smallest font on the computer to write it because he felt that what he had done was too terrible to be written down. But it usually seemed that when the kids started letting it out, it would just gush forth. I never considered that we made much progress until I had the confession letter in hand.

All of the boys were special to me, but one boy, I'll call him Jim, stood out in many ways. He was raised in a Pentecostal family and was a very sweet, loving young man. His story was that all of the people who hurt him his whole life were church people; other students in parochial schools and a church deacon who taught at one of the schools. This young man later worked at a Goodwill store and ran across a Satanic bible. He knew the Holy Bible inside out, but Christians were alienating him at every turn and it wasn't working, so he accepted the teachings of Anton LaVey.

Ouija Board (also has a heart shaped pointer)
(Courtesy Wikipedia/Wikimedia)[36]

According to his confession letter, one night he and a friend held a séance. He said everything was perfect. When he asked the Ouija board where the evil spirit resided, the pointer on the board moved without either of them touching it, and it spelled out his initials, J-A-T. Stunned that the pointer moved and spelled out his initials, he told the evil spirit to present itself.

Jim's buddy screamed as a wind in the basement blew out the candles. After they got the candles lit again, Jim asked why his buddy screamed. The buddy said that, just before the candles went out, Jim's face turned into the Devil.

Some time before Jim came to the school, he painted some fascinating and intriguing portraits and his parents sent them to the school. They were incredible and I think they could have hung in any art gallery. They were all done with dark gray and red paint on an off-white canvas paper. The eyes were mesmerizing. Usually there was one eye that was detailed and riveting and the other was assumed by a smear of dark gray and red paint. One picture was a self-portrait that was just a grimacing set of teeth with no eyes. It was pure agony. I just can't describe them enough; they were demonic, yet tantalizing.

Jim's father asked me to take the paintings to my preacher and ask him about them, so one night I took them home with me. The hair raised up on the back of my neck as I carried them to the car, and I prayed for protection to get safely home with them. The next night our friends, Connie and Raymond, came over and we had supper and played cards, 5-point pitch. I showed them the paintings and I was amazed at Connie's interpretation.

I've think that I've mentioned Connie before as being spiritual. Probably 15 years ago, when we were just becoming friends, Connie and Raymond visited some of their family in South Africa. After they returned from Africa, they had a terrible string of bad luck.

The classic Row Crop tractor (an Allis-Chalmers WD).

This is an old Allis-Chalmers WD. We had two of the next model, WD-45, when I was a kid. One was a gas and the other was a diesel. I think that it was the gas tractor that would vibrate and tickle your foot if you were riding on the back on the drawbar. The tractor pictured is probably just a little bit smaller than the one that ran over Raymond. Imagine the lugs on those back tires mashing you into the ground!

(Courtesy Wikipedia/Wikimedia)[37]

Raymond and his brother, Dean, farmed their mother's farm along with working their regular jobs. That spring, Dean was spreading fertilizer with an AC D-15 tractor pulling a fertilizer buggy in preparation for the spring planting. A fertilizer spreader is powered by the power take-off on the tractor and at the tractor's rated RPM's, like 1900 RPM's, throws fertilizer about 40 feet to each side. So to get an accurate application of fertilizer, Dean got off the tractor and stepped off 40 feet and made a mark where to make the next pass.

Raymond was wanting to talk to Dean, and the tractor was loud, running fast at the rated RPM, so he reached around and pushed the throttle to slow the engine speed so he could hear to talk above the engine noise. Unfortunately, Raymond hit the hand clutch instead of the throttle. This put the tractor in gear and it jumped forward, with Raymond standing in front of the big rear, drive wheel. The big, cleated tire ran over his right leg, knocking him down, then ran over his right side, and the right side of his head. The fertilizer spreader had a jack stand on the drawbar and it caught him, rolled him around, and the fertilizer spreader with about two tons of fertilizer ran over his left arm and the left side of his rib cage.

Dean didn't know what to do, so he caught the tractor first and shut it off before he went back to see the damage. Dean told me he knew that Raymond was dead, smashed into the freshly tilled soil, but then he saw an eye twitch. Dean said, "Don't move, your leg is broke." To that, Raymond replied in a weak, breathy voice, "That's not all."

When my wife Katie and I went to see Raymond at the hospital, all I remember is that his right eye looked like a ruby. It was just one big blood clot. All together, I think he had a broken right leg, a broken left arm, the blood clot on his eye, and a bunch of broken ribs on both sides. Raymond is huge and strong and tough. He almost makes John Wayne look wimpy at times, but how he survived that I will never know. Six months later he was back to work.

I'm not sure about the time frame, but some time after the tractor accident, Connie was standing at the sink doing dishes when she had a vision. In the vision, she saw her son, Todd, galloping on a horse and being thrown off on his head and breaking his neck. Connie prayed and prayed and asked for protection for Todd, but one day when she came home from town, her brother was leading the horse back to the barn. When she asked where Todd was, her brother told her that Todd was galloping his horse and the horse threw him on his head and it should have broken his neck, but the EMT's had taken him to the hospital and he seemed OK. He suffered no serious consequences.

Then some time later, Raymond was working in a hole in the ground fixing a drain tile problem. He told his son Todd to hit the steel post he was holding with a sledge hammer. Todd was young and hesitated, but Raymond said "hit it". And when Raymond says "hit it", you "hit it". So Todd swung and missed the steel post and hit Raymond in the head with the sledge hammer. Raymond crawled out of the hole before collapsing because he said he knew they'd never get him out of the pit if he collapsed in the hole. I don't think he had a skull fracture or nothing except for a big, throbbing pain in his head. Didn't even go to the doctor.

Like I mentioned earlier, this string of bad luck came after returning from a trip to Africa. On that trip, Connie brought home several native sculptures and figurines. One was a large marble elephant that she displayed prominently in the central room of the house. Now this is where it gets bizarre. One night Connie was home alone when she heard the vertical blinds rattle. When she looked up, she swears that she saw what appeared to be an African native with white paint on his face, vertical lines on one side of his face and horizontal lines on the other. Scared her to death. After all of the really bad luck and then this, they started to suspect the elephant statue in the house. Apparently there is a lot of voo-doo in Africa and they were afraid that they brought some home with them so they took the marble statue of the elephant out of the house and the preacher came and anointed it with oil. Coincidentally or not, the string of bad luck was broken.

This is all a lot of background to set the stage for the interpretation of the portraits. Jim's dad wanted me to show the paintings to my preacher, but I didn't need to. When Connie saw them she said it was obvious. All of the people were blinded, one eye or both in the case of the self-portrait. The swoosh that represented one of the eyes was first dark gray and then a swoosh of red paint over the top of the gray. Connie said the interpretation was obvious. The people were blinded by the gray and couldn't see the blood of Christ, the red paint on top.

WWWWOOOO!!!!! That made too much sense to me. It was so obvious. All of that pain and anguish that was portrayed in these painting because they lost sight of their salvation. Unbelievable, but now the rest of the story.

The next day I was at Ma and Pa's Restaurant eating lunch when a waitress got a phone call saying that there was an explosion in the chemistry room of the local high school and the school was on fire. Well, my son, Tim, is the chemistry teacher. So I headed five miles to Augusta where the high school was located. It was sunny and calm so I could easily see the smoke rising straight up in the air.

As I was rushing towards Augusta, I looked down at the speedometer and I was going 85 miles per hour. In 1991 I got a call from my mother and she said, "David, your dad's dead." I remember half way to Mom's house that I looked down and I was running 85 mph. I thought to myself, "Oh Lord, please don't make me have to put my son in a body bag like I did my dad." I frantically pulled up to the police officer that was blocking traffic and asked about my son. He said that everyone had gotten out safely.

fire bursts thru roof by 12:30 3-3-06

This picture shows the fire burning through the roof of the old part of the Augusta High School where I had chemistry and physics and biology when I was a kid. I think that my parents even had the same

127

teacher I had, Mrs. Emma Campbell. She was very strict and my wife
said that she favored the boys over the girls. HMMMM! Maybe? I
always just thought that I was a brown-noser.
Photo courtesy Rudy Kemppainen.[39]

I pulled up a little and stopped the truck. At that point, I
learned how it felt to wail uncontrollably. It's a combination of crying
and moaning and groaning, a sense of relief and thankfulness, and, at
the same time, extreme emotional pain. After a few moments of
wailing uncontrollably, when I got myself under control, I got out of
the truck and headed for the burning school building. They yelled at
me to stop, that I couldn't go up there, but at that point, I had so much
adrenaline pumping that no one was going to stop me without extreme
force.

When I got to the fire, I climbed up on the building and started
pulling on a fire hose and moving ladders. I helped the volunteers any
way I could until the Carthage Fire Department arrived with the big
ladder truck. They took over and told the untrained personnel to
vacate the area.

At that point, I went to find Tim who was supervising students
at the community center until their parents came or until they got on a
bus for home. When I first saw Tim and he was OK, I really don't
recall any emotion. I'm sure I was thankful, but I was wrung out. So,
everyone was safe and the school was totally destroyed.

The next morning I went to get in the car to go to work at the
boys' school. It was about 5:00 am and still very dark. When I opened
the car door, the dome light came on and instantly I saw the paintings
lying on the back seat of the car. Coincidence, I don't know. The
timing was absolutely perfect. You'll never convince me that there was
no connection between the fire and the paintings.

I reported Connie's interpretation of the pictures to Jim's
father. Apparently it made sense to him also. He requested that the
school destroy the paintings. Jim had told me that I could have my
choice of the paintings and I really, really wanted to keep one, but I
was too afraid to have one in my possession. The supervisors at the
academy ran the pictures through a paper shredder. I wasn't there, but
I've always wondered if they squealed as they were ground up.

I haven't seen Jim for a couple of years now. I often wonder how he is getting along. He was such a nice kid, but tormented so badly.

The Southeastern High School was rebuilt and the new facility was opened in the fall of 2008. I wouldn't have believed it. As I watched the old school burn that day, I thought that it was the day that the town of Augusta died, but I couldn't have been more wrong. With the insurance and some government assistance, a new $8 million facility was built. In a town of about 600, there will be something there for a long time.

Again, this seems pretty far out. I'll report and you decide.

For more information about Southeastern High School, look at www.southeastern337.com.

The Ol' Turkey Hunter

Tale #9
In the Beginning

as told by

"The Ol' Turkey Hunter"

Shown here many, many years ago on a Christmas Card with first wife Katie and son Tim before there were even any turkeys in the State of Illinois to hunt. Daughter Lorree wasn't born yet. That reminds me of a scary situation. Tim was born when I was 20, Lorree was born when I was 30, Nathan was born when I was 40, and one night when I was 50, Katie sent me out to get some ice cream and pickles. I about had a stroke.

The Ol' Turkey Hunter

In the Beginning

When I first started writing these short stories, I called the book Bazaar Short Stories of the Bible because it obviously consisted of some really strange short stories found in the Bible. However, after thinking about it a while, I decided that the word "Bible" turns many people off, so I decided to remove that from the name.

Then, when I was writing this chapter, "In the Beginning", I thought to myself, "Now, that's a unique thing, creation of the universe, kind of a bazaar event." So I questioned, what is bazaar.

When I looked it up on Wikipedia, the definition was; "a permanent merchandising area, **marketplace,** or street of shops where goods and services are exchanged or sold."

Well, bazaar was not what I wanted. I wanted the weird or strange meaning, an adjective. But there was none listed under bazaar. I wasn't sure of the correct spelling of the word when I started, but now I was sure I was spelling it incorrectly. I wanted to use the word that was descriptive of something that was odd or unusual, strikingly out of the ordinary. That word is spelled bizarre. I knew that once upon a time, but my memory isn't very good.

So I changed the name of the book to A Bazaar of Bizarre Short Stories. Pretty cool, I thought. But when I ran it past my friend Rudy, he said that bizarre sounds too gruesome, like having someone being cut up into pieces or something and he suggested something more appropriate like Tales of the Strange and Wonderful. HMMMMM???!!! That sounded pretty good.

So to continue with my previous train of thought, I found the creation of the universe to be bazaar, then bizarre, and finally, strange and truly wonderful. So now, let's get back to "In the Beginning".

Many people know the first verse of the Bible.

In the beginning God created the heavens and the earth.

Garden of eden by Cranach d. A. Lucas
(Courtesy Wikipedia/Wikimedia)[41]

Well, I'd say that the creation of the universe definitely qualifies as strikingly out of the ordinary. As I mentioned earlier, I really enjoy science. Science does really well with facts that can be proven, but I'm not so sure about some of the theory, like "The Big Bang" Theory. I went to get a definition for theory from Wikipedia, but I think the definition was written by someone a whole lot smarter than me because I didn't understand what he was saying, so, here's my simple definition of theory.

THEORY-I think this is what happened cause I wasn't there when it happened and I think this makes sense.

According to my definition of theory, "The Big Bang" Theory is really just "The Big Bang Guess" Theory or "The Big Bang Speculation" Theory. However, it is preached as gospel in public schools and colleges all across our country.

Big Bang by Cedric Sorel
I guess everyone has his own idea of the "Big Bang", but this reminds
me of something else everyone has one of.
(Courtesy Wikipedia/Wikimedia)[42]

And I always wonder what "banged" in "The Big Bang"
Theory. When I think about an explosion or "bang", I think of
dynamite, a gun, fireworks, a nuclear bomb, even a can of pressurized
hair spray. But it's always something physical that rapidly expands from
solid or liquid form, which is dense, to a gaseous form, which is a
vapor. So again, back to my question, what "banged"? Was it a black
hole? What makes a black hole black? Lots of guesses, I mean theories.

Recently Walter Cronkite died. I grew up listening to him on
TV on the evening news. As I listened to the tributes on CBS, they
showed his excitement with the launching of space rockets. I was
unaware that Cronkite was awarded a moon rock because of his
coverage and sincere interest in the space program.

As an aside, my Uncle Ernie was in charge of the fueling
operations for the Saturn V booster at Cape Kennedy. When I was a
senior in high school in 1969, our family went to Cocoa Beach, Florida,
to visit and Ernie gave us a guided tour of the facilities. That was
December just after Neil Armstrong first stepped on the moon the
previous July. The equipment and technology was incredible for 40
years ago.

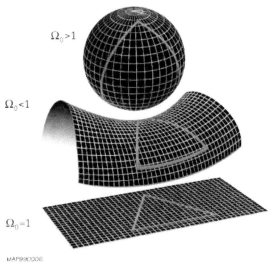

$\Omega_0 > 1$

$\Omega_0 < 1$

$\Omega_0 = 1$

MAP990006

Wikipedia says, "The overall geometry of the Universe is determined by whether the Omega cosmological parameter is less than, equal to or greater than 1. Shown from top to bottom are a closed Universe with positive curvature, a hyperbolic Universe with negative curvature and a flat Universe with zero curvature."
(Courtesy Wikipedia/Wikimedia)[43]

But back to the moon rock. The TV reported that scientists determined that the moon rocks are much older than Earth rocks. That makes an interesting theory. I figured that, according to "The Big Bang" Theory, that all rocks were made in the "Big Bang". I'd think that makes all rocks twins, born at the same time. But maybe the moon cooled off faster because it was smaller and that makes them older? I don't know, I wasn't there.

But let's go back and see what the Bible has to say about it.

In the beginning God created the heavens and the earth.

The earth was formless and void, and darkness was over the surface of the deep, and the Spirit of God was moving over the surface of the waters.

Then God said, "Let there be light"; and there was light. God saw that the light was good; and God separated the light from the darkness. God called the light day, and the darkness He called night. And there was evening and there was morning, one day.

Then God said, "Let there be an expanse in the midst of the waters, and let it separate the waters from the waters." God made the expanse, and separated the waters which were below the expanse from the waters which were above the expanse; and it was so. God called the expanse heaven. And there was evening and there was morning, a second day.

Then God said, "Let the waters below the heavens be gathered into one place, and let the dry land appear"; and it was so. God called the dry land earth, and the gathering of the waters He called seas; and God saw that it was good. Then God said, "Let the earth sprout vegetation, plants yielding seed, and fruit trees on the earth bearing fruit after their kind with seed in them"; and it was so. The earth brought forth vegetation, plants yielding seed after their kind, and trees bearing fruit with seed in them, after their kind; and God saw that it was good. There was evening and there was morning, a third day.

Then God said, "Let there be lights in the expanse of the heavens to separate the day from the night, and let them be for signs and for seasons and for days and years; and let them be for lights in the expanse of the heavens to give light on the earth"; and it was so. God made the two great lights, the greater light to govern the day, and the lesser light to govern the night; He made the stars also. God placed them in the expanse of the heavens to give light on the earth, and to govern the day and the night, and to separate the light from the darkness; and God saw that it was good. There was evening and there was morning, a fourth day.

Then God said, "Let the waters teem with swarms of living creatures, and let birds fly above the earth in the open expanse of the heavens." God created the great sea monsters and every living creature that moves, with which the waters swarmed after their kind, and every winged bird after its kind; and God saw that it was good. God blessed them, saying, "Be fruitful and multiply, and fill the waters in the seas, and let birds multiply on the earth." There was evening and there was morning, a fifth day.

Then God said, "Let the earth bring forth living creatures after their kind: cattle and creeping things and beasts of the earth after their kind"; and it was so. God made the beasts of the earth after their kind, and the cattle after their kind, and everything that creeps on the ground after its kind; and God saw that it was good. Then God said, "Let Us make man in Our image, according to Our likeness; and let them rule over the fish of the sea and over the birds of the sky and over the cattle and over all the earth, and over every creeping thing that creeps on the earth." God created man in His own image, in the image of God He created him; male and female He created them.

God blessed them; and God said to them, "Be fruitful and multiply, and fill the earth, and subdue it; and rule over the fish of the sea and over the birds of the sky and over every living thing that moves on the earth."

Then God said, "Behold, I have given you every plant yielding seed that is on the surface of all the earth, and every tree which has fruit yielding seed; it shall be food for you; and to every beast of the earth and to every bird of the sky and to every thing that moves on the earth which has life, I have given every green plant for food"; and it was so. God saw all that He had made, and behold, it was very good. And there was evening and there was morning, the sixth day.

Thus the heavens and the earth were completed, and all their hosts.

By the seventh day God completed His work which He had done, and He rested on the seventh day from all His work which He had done. Then God blessed the seventh day and sanctified it, because in it

He rested from all His work which God had created and made.

This is the account of how God created Creation. The following explains it in a little more detail.

This is the account of the heavens and the earth when they were created, in the day that the LORD God made earth and heaven.

Now no shrub of the field was yet in the earth, and no plant of the field had yet sprouted, for the LORD God had not sent rain upon the earth, and there was no man to cultivate the ground. But a mist used to rise from the earth and water the whole surface of the ground.

Then the LORD God formed man of dust from the ground, and breathed into his nostrils the breath of life; and man became a living being.

The LORD God planted a garden toward the east, in Eden; and there He placed the man whom He had formed.

Out of the ground the LORD God caused to grow every tree that is pleasing to the sight and good for food; the tree of life also in the midst of the garden, and the tree of the knowledge of good and evil.

Now a river flowed out of Eden to water the garden; and from there it divided and became four rivers. The name of the first is Pishon; it flows around the whole land of Havilah, where there is gold. The gold of that land is good; the bdellium and the onyx stone are there.

The name of the second river is Gihon; it flows around the whole land of Cush. The name of the third river is tigris; it flows east of Assyria And the fourth river is the Euphrates.

Then the LORD God took the man and put him into the garden of Eden to cultivate it and keep it. The LORD God commanded the man, saying, "From any tree of the garden you may eat freely; but from the tree of the knowledge of good and evil you shall not eat, for in the day that you eat from it you will surely die."

Then the LORD God said, "It is not good for the man to be alone; I will make him a helper suitable for him." Out of the ground the LORD God formed every beast of the field and every bird of the sky, and brought them to the man to see what he would call them; and whatever the man called a living creature, that was its name.

Lucas Cranach the Elder (1472-1553):
Adam and Eve.
(Courtesy Wikipedia/Wikimedia)[44]

The man gave names to all the cattle, and to the birds of the sky, and to every beast of the field, but for Adam there was not found a helper suitable for him.

So the LORD God caused a deep sleep to fall upon the man, and he slept; then He took one of his ribs and closed up the flesh at that place. The LORD God fashioned into a woman the rib which He had taken from the man, and brought her to the man.

The man said, This is now bone of my bones, And flesh of my flesh; She shall be called Woman, Because she was taken out of Man."

For this reason a man shall leave his father and his mother, and be joined to his wife; and they shall become one flesh.

And the man and his wife were both naked and were not ashamed.

God took a rib out of the man and made a woman, a helper for Adam. I heard that Adam did some negotiating with God about this helper. Now, understand that this is just theory.

Adam told God that he wanted someone that was a great cook, kept a very neat and clean house, and took care of the kids and the crops, etc, etc, etc. God pondered this request for some time. The next time he met Adam in the Garden of Eden, He agreed to grant Adam's request for a helper, but added, "OK, but that's going to cost you an arm and a leg." Adam looked at his fingers and then wiggled his toes and asked, "What can I get for a rib?"

But seriously. If God took a rib out of a man, men should have 12 ribs on one side and 11 ribs on the other side. I don't remember where, but several years ago I read an article about a man who had an injury or cancer or something and doctors took out his lowest rib on one side. Some years later, X-rays showed that the rib had regenerated or grown back. My jaw dropped when I read that. I know you can cut a worm in half and they grow back, but a rib? This is just something I read a long time ago, so don't hold me to it as being factual.

But my dad's finger never grew back. During harvest one year, he jumped off the side of our two-ton truck that we used to haul grain to the elevator. His wedding ring caught on the top as he jumped. The ring didn't just slide off. No, first the band pinched together and then pealed the meat off the bone of his ring finger, just like when you skin out the tail of a raccoon. The doctors took off the bone and remaining

Adam and eve by Lucas Cranach

As I look at these paintings of Adam and Eve, I somewhat question their accuracy. They all have belly buttons. A belly button is the point of attachment of the umbilical cord and the placenta. If God made Adam and Eve out of the dust, did they have belly buttons?

(Courtesy Wikipedia/Wikimedia)[45]

meat at the joint where the finger meets the hand. That finger never grew back, but it was strange that Dad often had the sensation of

142

having dirt under that fingernail which was no longer there. I think they call that a "phantom pain".

On the news the other day, I saw where a company from England grew human sperm cells from embryonic stem cells. It seems that when you subject embryonic cells to different hormones and chemicals, they develop into different types of cells. Think about it, ½ of a man's cell plus ½ of a woman's cell results in a baby. I think all babies, boys and girls, start out the same way until the hormones of the fetus kick in and the sex of the baby is then determined. Again, you start with ½ of a man's cell and ½ of a woman's cell and that cell divides and makes two cells and they divide and make four cells and so on. It would make sense that this cell division would make a blob of cells with the same characteristics. But as we all know, from these original cells, some become muscle cells and some become blood cells, some brain cells and some bone cells. How can that be? Sounds like intelligent design to me.

I was thinking about how to design the family tree of a cloned individual. I think I finally decide that it would have to include a straight line somewhere, but my head was hurting so I quit thinking about it.

Family trees are getting very bizarre these days. My wife used to babysit for a little girl, and the girl's mother made the comment one time, "I always wondered who my mother-in-law would be, but I never dreamed it would be my sister!" It hurts my head thinking about how to diagram that family tree.

It's pretty interesting to see how babies develop, especially baby birds. If you ever break an egg and see a developing bird embryo, you will notice that the eyes are very large in proportion to the rest of the bird. I think the reason for this is because the eyes are so intricate that they need more time to develop. How could eyes and vision randomly develop from the slime in a marsh? Eyes don't really see things like we often think, they actually translate light into electrical impulses in the nerves that our brains can use to create a picture. I've seen where scientists can imitate sight with a camera that they hook up to a blind person's optical nerve and the blind person can distinguish between a large number 1 and a large number 2. I think that someday they may be able to overcome blindness to a certain degree by hooking a camera up to the optic nerve.

I don't think that they have created a baby from these engineered, embryonic stem cells turned sperm yet, but I'm sure that is in the plans. It seems that there is no end to what science can create. I heard a story about what advancements science has made. This may be a theory.

The top scientists in the world challenged God to see who could make the most perfect human being. The scientists made the rules. Each team was given one year to engineer a perfect human. All they had to start with was 100 pounds of red Georgia clay.

Agrinomically speaking, soil is made of three different size particles. Sand is the most coarse. When it gets weathered and ground down into smaller particles, it is called silt. And the smallest soil particles are called clay. Clay particles fit closely together and usually restrict water penetration compared to sand or silt. Some of the most productive farmland is called loam, which is a combination of soil particle sizes, like a sandy loam, or silty clay loam.

The day for the start of the competition finally arrived and the scientists were confident and all excited to show up God; to show him that they could create a better man than He could. As the competition was getting ready to start, God asked if the scientists really wanted to make the competition fair. Feeling pretty confident and cocky, they agreed to a rules adjustment to make the competition fair.

So God said, "MAKE YOUR OWN DIRT!!!!!"

To learn more about the creation, read in Genesis.

Tale #10

Do you know

Mr. Ed's Uncle?

as told by

"The Ol' Turkey Hunter"

Shown here in his younger days as a draft animal out on the farm.

The Ol' Turkey Hunter

Do you know
Mr. Ed's Uncle?

I was raised on a farm, but we never had horses or donkeys or mules. In fact, I know the difference between a donkey and a mule, but I always forget which is which. One is a pure species and the other is a true hybrid.

A donkey at Clovelly, The One the Only,
England.
Taken by Adrian Pingstone in July 2004
(Courtesy Wikipedia/Wikimedia)[46]

Wikipedia says, "The donkey or ass, Equus africanus asinus. (I wonder if that's where the word asinine comes from?) A male donkey or ass is called a jack, (alas, my wife's unaffectionate nickname for me, jack ass) a female a jenny, and offspring less than one year old, a foal.
While different species of the Equidae family can interbreed, offspring are almost always sterile. Nonetheless, horse/donkey hybrids

147

are popular for their durability and vigor. A mule is the offspring of a jack (male donkey) and a mare (female horse). The much rarer successful mating of a male horse and a female donkey produces a hinny."

The reason mules are sterile is due to the fact that horses and donkeys have a different number of chromosomes in the cells that make up their body. God made like to beget like. In the case of a mule, that does not happen because a mule is a true hybrid, so the resulting offspring is sterile and cannot reproduce. We are told not to be unequally yoked, and it looks like that applies even in the basic cell.

This pair of mules were working a plowing exhibition at The Farnsley-Moreman House in Louisville, Kentucky
Author Joe Schneid Louisville, KY
(Courtesy Wikipedia/Wikimedia)[47]

When geneticists speak of hybrid corn, it is a cross between two pure lines (different families, but the same genus with the same number of pairs of chromosomes) and not between two species (like crossing corn with wheat). The first cross between separate pure line families gives the offspring an advantage in vigor being stronger than either of the two parent lines, a phenomenon referred to as hybrid vigor. Hybrid vigor plays a big part in the advances of modern agriculture, especially in corn production and swine production.

I'm sure Mark Twain knew all about the Missouri Mule. They are legendary for their strength and stamina and versatility and contrariety. Mules are better than 4-wheelers for coon hunters. They are sure footed and when you come to a fence, just lay your coat over the wires, jump the mule over the fence, and continue the chase. Back in the day, they were used for transportation and pulling a plow.

An intent donkeyball player eyes the basket. I think they gave her a well behaved and cooperative donkey. (Courtesy Wikipedia/Wikimedia)[48]

I never did know what donkeys were good for except to make mules. An unusual use but very popular in our area is Donkey Basketball. They put rubber shoes on the donkeys so they don't scuff the floor and local celebrities put on a spectacle trying to play basketball while riding the donkeys. The players find very quickly that the donkeys have a mind of their own and many of the "rides" are selected because of a certain quirk that is entertaining to the crowd.

I've found that a lot of stories and ideas of today have their roots in the Bible. Mr. Ed was a very popular TV show when I was a kid growing up. The idea of a horse that was smart and would talk like any other person was so ridiculous that it was hysterical. I laughed and laughed, but I didn't know that Mr. Ed had relatives that could talk back in Bible days.

A Palomino Horse
All of the pictures of Mr. Ed that I could find were copywrited so I finally found this nice horse picture to use in it's place. This horse could possibly be Mr. Ed's grandson or great-grandson, but I doubt it. Mr. Ed was probably a gelding. (Courtesy Wikipedia/Wikimedia)[49]

Mr. Ed was best on the phone so he didn't have to explain his appearance or the fact that he was a talking horse. As you probably know, Mr. Ed would never speak unless he had something to say.

Well, Balaam's donkey was about the same as Mr. Ed. He only spoke once, but he had something very important to say. Let's see what happened.

Then the sons of Israel journeyed, and camped in the plains of Moab beyond the Jordan opposite Jericho. Now Balak the son of Zippor saw all that Israel had done to the Amorites (*they destroyed them in battle*). So Moab was in great fear because of the people, for they were numerous; and Moab was in dread of the sons of Israel.

150

Moab said to the elders of Midian, "Now this horde will lick up all that is around us, as the ox licks up the grass of the field."

And Balak the son of Zippor was king of Moab at that time. So he sent messengers to Balaam the son of Beor, at Pethor, which is near the River, in the land of the sons of his people, to call him, saying, "Behold, a people came out of Egypt; behold, they cover the surface of the land, and they are living opposite me. Now, therefore, please come, curse this people for me since they are too mighty for me; perhaps I may be able to defeat them and drive them out of the land. For I know that he whom you bless is blessed, and he whom you curse is cursed."

So the elders of Moab and the elders of Midian departed with the fees for divination in their hand; and they came to Balaam and repeated Balak's words to him. He **(Balaam)** said to them, "Spend the night here, and I will bring word back to you as the LORD may speak to me." And the leaders of Moab stayed with Balaam.

Then God came to Balaam and said, "Who are these men with you?" Balaam said to God, "Balak the son of Zippor, king of Moab, has sent word to me, 'Behold, there is a people who came out of Egypt and they cover the surface of the land; now come, curse them for me; perhaps I may be able to fight against them and drive them out.'"

God said to Balaam, "Do not go with them; you shall not curse the people, for they are blessed." So Balaam arose in the morning and said to Balak's leaders, "Go back to your land, for the LORD has refused to let me go with you."

The leaders of Moab arose and went to Balak and said, "Balaam refused to come with us." Then Balak again sent leaders, more numerous and more distinguished than the former. They came to Balaam and said to him, "Thus says Balak the son of Zippor,

'Let nothing, I beg you, hinder you from coming to me; for I will indeed honor you richly, and I will do whatever you say to me. Please come then, curse this people for me.'"

Balaam replied to the servants of Balak, "Though Balak were to give me his house full of silver and gold, I could not do anything, either small or great, contrary to the command of the LORD my God.

"Now please, you also stay here tonight, and I will find out what else the LORD will speak to me." God came to Balaam at night and said to him, "If the men have come to call you, rise up and go with them; but only the word which I speak to you shall you do."

So Balaam arose in the morning, and saddled his donkey and went with the leaders of Moab. But God was angry because he was going, and the angel of the LORD took his stand in the way as an adversary against him. Now he was riding on his donkey and his two servants were with him.

When the donkey saw the angel of the LORD standing in the way with his drawn sword in his hand, the donkey turned off from the way and went into the field; but Balaam struck the donkey to turn her back into the way.

Then the angel of the LORD stood in a narrow path of the vineyards, with a wall on this side and a wall on that side. When the donkey saw the angel of the LORD, she pressed herself to the wall and pressed Balaam's foot against the wall, so he struck her again.

The angel of the LORD went further, and stood in a narrow place where there was no way to turn to the right hand or the left. When the donkey saw the angel of the LORD, she lay down under Balaam; so Balaam was angry and struck the donkey with his stick.

Balaam and his Ass.
Rembrandt van Rijn (1606, Leiden – 1669, Amsterdam)
(Courtesy Wikipedia/Wikimedia)[50]

That reminds me of the old farmer that was leading his mule down the road, when the mule laid down and wouldn't move, so, like Balaam, he swatted the mule with a whip, all to no avail. The mule just laid there.

A passer-by stopped to help the farmer with the mule. He said, "Don't whip him like that. You have to be nice and coax him to go with you." So the passer-by picked up a 2x4 and smacked the mule in the head with it. The stunned farmer exclaimed, "I thought you said that you had to be nice to the mule." The passer-bye said, "You do. But you got to get his attention first."

And the LORD opened the mouth of the donkey, and she said to Balaam, "What have I done to you, that you have struck me these three times?"

Then Balaam said to the donkey, "Because you have made a mockery of me! If there had been a sword in my hand, I would have killed you by now."

The donkey said to Balaam, "Am I not your donkey on which you have ridden all your life to this day? Have I ever been accustomed to do so to you?" And he said, "No." Then the LORD opened the eyes of Balaam, and he saw the angel of the LORD standing in the way with his drawn sword in his hand; and he bowed all the way to the ground.

The angel of the LORD said to him, "Why have you struck your donkey these three times? Behold, I have come out as an adversary, because your way was contrary to me. But the donkey saw me and turned aside from me these three times. If she had not turned aside from me, I would surely have killed you just now, and let her live."

Balaam said to the angel of the LORD, "I have sinned, for I did not know that you were standing in the way against me. Now then, if it is displeasing to you, I will turn back." But the angel of the LORD said to Balaam, "Go with the men, but you shall speak only the word which I tell you." So Balaam went along with the leaders of Balak.

Sometimes people get caught up in the moment and go along with the crowd instead of standing their ground. I think that God wanted to make sure that Balaam didn't weaken and curse the Israelites, so this was his way of "getting Balaam's attention".

When Balak heard that Balaam was coming, he went out to meet him at the city of Moab, which is on the Arnon border, at the extreme end of the border. Then Balak said to Balaam, "Did I not urgently send to you to call you? Why did you not come to me? Am I really unable to honor you?"

So Balaam said to Balak, "Behold, I have come now to you! Am I able to speak anything at all? The word that God puts in my mouth, that I shall speak." And Balaam went with Balak, and they came to Kiriath-huzoth. Balak sacrificed oxen and sheep, and sent some to Balaam and the leaders who were with him.

Then it came about in the morning that Balak took Balaam and brought him up to the high places of Baal, and he saw from there a portion of the people. Then Balaam said to Balak, "Build seven altars for me here, and prepare seven bulls and seven rams for me here."

I've heard that 7 is God's number, it took 6 days to create the universe and the 7th was God's day. I've also heard that 6 is the Devil's number, because it leaves out the seventh day, God's day of rest. Maybe that's why Balaam requested seven altars.

Picture of altar

Wikipedia says, "Detail of Religion mural in lunette from the Family and Education series by Charles Sprague Pearce. North Corridor, Great Hall, Library of Congress Thomas Jefferson Building, Washington, D.C. Mural contains artist's logo and "COPYRIGHT 1896 BY C.S.PEARCE"."

(Courtesy Wikipedia/Wikimedia)[51]

Balak did just as Balaam had spoken, and Balak and Balaam offered up a bull and a ram on each altar.

Then Balaam said to Balak, "Stand beside your burnt offering, and I will go; perhaps the LORD will come to meet me, and whatever He shows me I will tell you." So he went to a bare hill.

Now God met Balaam, and he said to Him, "I have set up the seven altars, and I have offered up a bull and a ram on each altar." Then the LORD put a word in Balaam's mouth and said, "Return to Balak, and you shall speak thus." So he returned to him, and behold, he was standing beside his burnt offering, he and all the leaders of Moab. He took up his discourse and said,

"From Aram Balak has brought me,
Moab's king from the mountains of the East,
'Come curse Jacob for me,
And come, denounce Israel!'
"How shall I curse whom God has not cursed?
And how can I denounce whom the LORD has not denounced?
"As I see him from the top of the rocks,
And I look at him from the hills;
Behold, a people who dwells apart,
And will not be reckoned among the nations.
"Who can count the dust of Jacob,
Or number the fourth part of Israel?
Let me die the death of the upright,
And let my end be like his!"

Then Balak said to Balaam, "What have you done to me? I took you to curse my enemies, but behold, you have actually blessed them!" He replied, "Must I not be careful to speak what the LORD puts in my mouth?"

Then Balak said to him, "Please come with me to another place from where you may see them, although you will only see the extreme end of them and will not see all of them; and curse them for me from there."

So he took him to the field of Zophim, to the top of Pisgah, and built seven altars and offered a bull

and a ram on each altar. And he said to Balak, "Stand
here beside your burnt offering while I myself meet the
LORD over there."

Then the LORD met Balaam and put a word in
his mouth and said, "Return to Balak, and thus you
shall speak." He came to him, and behold, he was
standing beside his burnt offering, and the leaders of
Moab with him. And Balak said to him, "What has the
LORD spoken?" Then he took up his discourse and
said,
"Arise, O Balak, and hear;
Give ear to me, O son of Zippor!
"God is not a man, that He should lie,
Nor a son of man, that He should repent;
Has He said, and will He not do it?
Or has He spoken, and will He not make it good?
"Behold, I have received a command to bless;
When He has blessed, then I cannot revoke it.
"He has not observed misfortune in Jacob;
Nor has He seen trouble in Israel;
The LORD his God is with him,
And the shout of a king is among them.
"God brings them out of Egypt,
He is for them like the horns of the wild ox.
"For there is no omen against Jacob,
Nor is there any divination against Israel;
At the proper time it shall be said to Jacob
And to Israel, what God has done!
"Behold, a people rises like a lioness,
And as a lion it lifts itself;
It will not lie down until it devours the prey,
And drinks the blood of the slain."

With guts like that, it's no wonder so many of the prophets
died untimely deaths.

Then Balak said to Balaam, "Do not curse them
at all nor bless them at all!" But Balaam replied to

Balak, "Did I not tell you, 'Whatever the LORD speaks, that I must do'?"

Then Balak said to Balaam, "Please come, I will take you to another place; perhaps it will be agreeable with God that you curse them for me from there." So Balak took Balaam to the top of Peor which overlooks the wasteland. Balaam said to Balak, "Build seven altars for me here and prepare seven bulls and seven rams for me here." Balak did just as Balaam had said, and offered up a bull and a ram on each altar.

When Balaam saw that it pleased the LORD to bless Israel, he did not go as at other times to seek omens but he set his face toward the wilderness. And Balaam lifted up his eyes and saw Israel camping tribe by tribe; and the Spirit of God came upon him. He took up his discourse and said,

"The oracle of Balaam the son of Beor,
And the oracle of the man whose eye is opened;
The oracle of him who hears the words of God,
Who sees the vision of the Almighty,
Falling down, yet having his eyes uncovered,
How fair are your tents, O Jacob,
Your dwellings, O Israel!
"Like valleys that stretch out,
Like gardens beside the river,
Like aloes planted by the LORD,
Like cedars beside the waters.
"Water will flow from his buckets,
And his seed will be by many waters,
And his king shall be higher than Agag,   And his
kingdom shall be exalted.
"God brings him out of Egypt,
He is for him like the horns of the wild ox
He will devour the nations who are his adversaries,
And will crush their bones in pieces,
And shatter them with his arrows.

"He crouches, he lies down as a lion,
And as a lion, who dares rouse him?
Blessed is everyone who blesses you,
And cursed is everyone who curses you."

Then Balak's anger burned against Balaam, and he struck his hands together; and Balak said to Balaam, "I called you to curse my enemies, but behold, you have persisted in blessing them these three times! Therefore, flee to your place now. I said I would honor you greatly, but behold, the LORD has held you back from honor."

Balaam said to Balak, "Did I not tell your messengers whom you had sent to me, saying, 'Though Balak were to give me his house full of silver and gold, I could not do anything contrary to the command of the LORD, either good or bad, of my own accord What the LORD speaks, that I will speak'? And now, behold, I am going to my people; come, and I will advise you what this people will do to your people in the days to come." He took up his discourse and said,

"The oracle of Balaam the son of Beor,
And the oracle of the man whose eye is opened,
The oracle of him who hears the words of God,
And knows the knowledge of the Most High,
Who sees the vision of the Almighty,
Falling down, yet having his eyes uncovered.
"I see him, but not now;
I behold him, but not near;
A star shall come forth from Jacob,
A scepter shall rise from Israel,
And shall crush through the forehead of Moab,
And tear down all the sons of Sheth.
"Edom shall be a possession,
Seir, its enemies, also will be a possession,
While Israel performs valiantly.
"One from Jacob shall have dominion,
And will destroy the remnant from the city."
Sounds like a prophecy predicting Christmas.

And he looked at Amalek and took up his discourse and said,

"Amalek was the first of the nations,
But his end shall be destruction."
And he looked at the Kenite, and took up his discourse
and said,
"Your dwelling place is enduring,
And your nest is set in the cliff.
Nevertheless Kain will be consumed;
How long will Asshur keep you captive?"
Then he took up his discourse and said,
"Alas, who can live except God has ordained it?
But ships shall come from the coast of Kittim,
And they shall afflict Asshur and will afflict Eber; So
they also will come to destruction." Then Balaam arose
and departed and returned to his place, and Balak also
went his way.

Now, I can't imagine the ruler of Iraq or Iran or Afghanistan or any of those countries calling me and telling me to curse the enemy and then bless them instead. You would have to have a death wish or the peace that passes understanding from God to be able to do such a thing.

And when you arose and departed, I'd be waiting for a bullet in the back, but he obviously benefitted from divine protection.

To learn more about Mr. Ed's uncle, read Numbers 22, 23, and 24. There's even more to the story in the next few chapters.

Tale #11
Drink like a Dog

as told by

"The Ol' Turkey Hunter"

Shown here working with a litter of English Setter pups. Their natural instinct is to point out birds for the hunter in the field. A point is actually an extended crouch before jumping upon the prey. These young pups are displaying that natural style and instinct as they point at a bird wing on a fishing pole.

The Ol' Turkey Hunter

Drink like a Dog

Talk about a broken record. Huh! That reminds me, did you ever notice that you never hear the music of a scratched record anymore? Music that repeats itself over and over and over and over until you touch the needle of the record player to help move the needle out of the groove that it is stuck in? Probably most young people have no idea what I'm talking about, but those who grew up with Elvis and the Beach Boys and the Beatles, and the generation before me with Lawrence Welk and Guy Lombardo, they do know what I'm talking about. And history seems to repeat itself just like a scratched record.

It didn't take long to get tired of a scratched record playing the same thing over and over, and you know what, I get kind of tired of the Israelites in the Bible doing the same things over and over and over. I can't imagine how frustrated God gets. You'd think they (we) would learn, but I guess people are people. Proud, arrogant, stupid.

Before Israel demanded a king, God sent special people (judges) to help the Israelites with their problems which usually included some form of fighting or disagreement. To this day, the Jewish people are known as being very intelligent and fierce fighters. Is that because they are good, or is it because God is protecting a remnant as he promised? Probably both, how should I know?

At the time of Gideon, Israel was deeply involved in idol worship and lots of other things that voided their covenant with God. The concept of consequences for our actions seems to be a foreign idea to the people of the world today as it was in the past, but there are consequences for our actions even today as there were in days of old.

Hah! or LOL. I saw in the newspaper where they were calling for more oversight for cemeteries. Oversight for cemeteries!!! Can you believe that? In Chicago, of course, managers of cemeteries were selling plots that already had dead people buried in them. In our day of legislation and litigation and blah, blah, blah, more rules ain't gonna make no difference. Morality and fear of being shamed is what keeps people in check, not some government schmoe that doesn't want to make waves and jeopardize his job. In other words, as my brother Bob says, "Suck the social sow." How many times do we have to hear that broken record again?

And while I'm talking about cemeteries, as I drove past our local cemetery, I saw an American Flag laying along the ditch. It was chopped up and laying in the dust. I backed up and retrieved it and put it in my truck so I could retire it at the American Legion. Obviously, the person mowing the cemetery was too lazy or more likely too apathetic to pick it up, so he just ran over it with the mower and left it. Maybe I'm just as apathetic as he is. I probably should have looked him up and beat the crap out of him, but I don't think that would have done much good, the public apathy is so great. That would never have happened when I was a kid.

But back to Gideon. It seems that God chooses humble people for some of his big projects. Gideon was a person of low standing in one of the smallest tribes of Joseph, so when he got the call, he couldn't believe it. He had to have three tests of God before he could believe it, but after the tests confirmed that God was involved, he was unwavering. Let's check out his story.

Then the sons of Israel did what was evil in the sight of the LORD; and the LORD gave them into the hands of Midian seven years.

The power of Midian prevailed against Israel. Because of Midian the sons of Israel made for themselves the dens which were in the mountains and the caves and the strongholds. For it was when Israel had sown, that the Midianites would come up with the Amalekites and the sons of the east and go against them. So they would camp against them and destroy the produce of the earth as far as Gaza, and leave no sustenance in Israel as well as no sheep, ox, or donkey. For they would come up with their livestock and their tents, they would come in like locusts for number, both they and their camels were innumerable; and they came into the land to devastate it. So Israel was brought very low because of Midian, and the sons of Israel cried to the LORD.

Basics of life, food, shelter, and water. Take away any one of these and the population drops. In our rural area, there used to be lots of ditches and briars and trees and brush, good places for quail to live. Today, with modern farming practices and erosion controls, the broken landscape is cleared and replaced with dry dams, plastic drain tiles and fescue grass to conserve the soil.

A brushy ditch where wildlife flourishes.

The brushy draw pictured on the previous page is on my brother's farm. It is good cover for wildlife even if it isn't an active draw. There is a pond at the end of the ditch that is checking any new erosion.

In an active draw, the ditch washes out a little more each year which creates a new edge of foxtail and small weeds followed by a strip of horseweeds, then briars, then small trees, and finally large trees. Many animals like this diversity (smorgasboard) of cover and foods.

Photo by Author.

165

This was a brushy draw very similar to the one pictured above, but it obviously has some differences now. All of the trees and weeds and plants that offered food and shelter to a host of animals just days ago is now totally barren. If the brush piles were left intact, they would eventually offer some shelter to rabbits and small birds, but these piles will be burned and the rest will be buried, leaving the draw looking like the one in the following picture.

Photo by author.

This was an active draw that supported much wildlife. Now it is blocked with a common soil conservation practice called a dry dam. All of the brush and trees are removed and a dam is formed across the ditch. Then the pond that is created by the dam is tiled out with plastic tile to keep it dry. Then the area is grassed down to prevent any further erosion. Dry dams are relatively inexpensive and very effective for controlling erosion, but hard on wildlife habitat.

Photo by Author.

Nothing likes to eat fescue. It has absolutely no nutritional value to quails and provides no protection, and today there are very few Bob Whites as compared to in the past. And that's what Sherman did in the Civil War. An extremely cruel and punishing, but very effective, tactic. Take away your Wal-Mart and Hy-Vee and see how you like it.

There are lots of big and unusual names in this passage. Don't let that confuse you.

Now it came about when the sons of Israel cried to the LORD on account of Midian, that the LORD sent a prophet to the sons of Israel, and he said to them, "Thus says the LORD, the God of Israel, 'It was I who brought you up from Egypt and brought you out from the house of slavery. I delivered you from the hands of the Egyptians and from the hands of all your oppressors, and dispossessed them before you and gave you their land, and I said to you, "I am the LORD your God; you shall not fear the gods of the Amorites in whose land you live. But you have not obeyed Me.""'"

Then the angel of the LORD came and sat under the oak that was in Ophrah, which belonged to Joash the Abiezrite as his son Gideon was beating out wheat in the wine press in order to save it from the Midianites.

The angel of the LORD appeared to him and said to him, "The LORD is with you, O valiant warrior." Then Gideon said to him, "O my lord, if the LORD is with us, why then has all this happened to us? And where are all His miracles which our fathers told us about, saying, 'Did not the LORD bring us up from Egypt?' But now the LORD has abandoned us and given us into the hand of Midian." The LORD looked at him and said, "Go in this your strength and deliver Israel from the hand of Midian. Have I not sent you?"

He said to Him, "O Lord, how shall I deliver Israel? Behold, my family is the least in Manasseh, and I am the youngest in my father's house." But the LORD said to him, "Surely I will be with you, and you shall defeat Midian as one man."

So Gideon said to Him, "If now I have found favor in Your sight, then show me a sign that it is You who speak with me. Please do not depart from here, until I come back to You, and bring out my offering and lay it before You." And He said, "I will remain until you return."

Then Gideon went in and prepared a young goat and unleavened bread from an ephah of flour; he put the meat in a basket and the broth in a pot, and brought them out to him under the oak and presented them. The angel of God said to him, "Take the meat and the unleavened bread and lay them on this rock, and pour out the broth." And he did so.

Then the angel of the LORD put out the end of the staff that was in his hand and touched the meat and the unleavened bread; and fire sprang up from the rock and consumed the meat and the unleavened bread. Then the angel of the LORD vanished from his sight.

When Gideon saw that he was the angel of the LORD, he said, "Alas, O Lord GOD! For now I have seen the angel of the LORD face to face." The LORD said to him, "Peace to you, do not fear; you shall not die." Then Gideon built an altar there to the LORD and named it The LORD is Peace. To this day it is still in Ophrah of the Abiezrites.

Now on the same night the LORD said to him, "Take your father's bull and a second bull seven years old, and pull down the altar of Baal which belongs to your father, and cut down the Asherah that is beside it; and build an altar to the LORD your God on the top of this stronghold in an orderly manner, and take a second bull and offer a burnt offering with the wood of the Asherah which you shall cut down."

Then Gideon took ten men of his servants and did as the LORD had spoken to him; and because he was too afraid of his father's household and the men of the city to do it by day, he did it by night.

Baal, right arm raised. Bronze figurine, 14th-12th centuries, found in Ras Shamra (ancient Ugarit).
(Courtesy Wikipedia/Wikimedia)[52]

Wikipedia says, " Ba'?al... is a Northwest Semitic title and honorific meaning "master" or "lord" that is used for various gods."

Earlier I said I thought people were proud, arrogant, and stupid. Talk about stupid. Who would call the little guy in the clown hat "master"?

And Wikipedia says "An Asherah pole is a sacred tree or pole that stood near Canaanite religious locations to honor the Ugaritic mother-goddess Asherah. Asherah is sometimes referred to as the Queen of Heaven."

In Jeremiah 7:18: *"The children gather wood, the fathers light the fire, and the women knead the dough and make cakes of bread for the Queen of Heaven. They pour out drink offerings to other gods to provoke me to anger."*

The next morning after Gideon tore down the idols,

When the men of the city arose early in the morning, behold, the altar of Baal was torn down, and the Asherah which was beside it was cut down, and the second bull was offered on the altar which had been built. They said to one another, "Who did this thing?" And when they searched about and inquired, they said, "Gideon the son of Joash did this thing."

Then the men of the city said to Joash, "Bring out your son, that he may die, for he has torn down the altar of Baal, and indeed, he has cut down the Asherah which was beside it." But Joash said to all who stood against him, "Will you contend for Baal, or will you deliver him? Whoever will plead for him shall be put to death by morning. If he is a god, let him contend for himself, because someone has torn down his altar." Therefore on that day he named him Jerubbaal, that is to say, "Let Baal contend against him," because he had torn down his altar.

Then all the Midianites and the Amalekites and the sons of the east assembled themselves; and they crossed over and camped in the valley of Jezreel. So the Spirit of the LORD came upon Gideon; and he blew a trumpet, and the Abiezrites were called together to follow him. He sent messengers throughout Manasseh, and they also were called together to follow him; and he sent messengers to Asher, Zebulun, and Naphtali, and they came up to meet them.

Then Gideon said to God, "If You will deliver Israel through me, as You have spoken,
behold, I will put a fleece of wool on the threshing floor. If there is dew on the fleece only, and it is dry on all the ground, then I will know that You will deliver Israel through me, as You have spoken." And it was so. When he arose early the next morning and squeezed the fleece, he drained the dew from the fleece, a bowl full of water.

Fine Merino shearing Lismore, Victoria
(Courtesy Wikipedia/Wikimedia)[53]

Then Gideon said to God, "Do not let Your anger burn against me that I may speak once more; please let me make a test once more with the fleece, let it now be dry only on the fleece, and let there be dew on all the ground."

God did so that night; for it was dry only on the fleece, and dew was on all the ground.

Then Jerubbaal (that is, Gideon) and all the people who were with him, rose early and camped beside the spring of Harod; and the camp of Midian was on the north side of them by the hill of Moreh in the valley. The LORD said to Gideon, "The people who are with you are too many for Me to give Midian into their hands, for Israel would become boastful, saying, 'My own power has delivered me.' "Now therefore come, proclaim in the hearing of the people, saying, 'Whoever is afraid and trembling, let him return and depart from Mount Gilead.'" So 22,000 people returned, but 10,000 remained. Then the LORD said to Gideon, "The people are still too many; bring them

171

down to the water and I will test them for you there. Therefore it shall be that he of whom I say to you, 'This one shall go with you,' he shall go with you; but everyone of whom I say to you, 'This one shall not go with you,' he shall not go."

So he brought the people down to the water. And the LORD said to Gideon, "You shall separate everyone who laps the water with his tongue as a dog laps, as well as everyone who kneels to drink." Now the number of those who lapped, putting their hand to their mouth, was 300 men; but all the rest of the people kneeled to drink water.

The LORD said to Gideon, "I will deliver you with the 300 men who lapped and will give the Midianites into your hands; so let all the other people go, each man to his home." So the 300 men took the people's provisions and their trumpets into their hands. And Gideon sent all the other men of Israel, each to his tent, but retained the 300 men; and the camp of Midian was below him in the valley.

Now the same night it came about that the LORD said to him, "Arise, go down against the camp, for I have given it into your hands. But if you are afraid to go down, go with Purah your servant down to the camp, and you will hear what they say; and afterward your hands will be strengthened that you may go down against the camp." So he went with Purah his servant down to the outposts of the army that was in the camp.

Now the Midianites and the Amalekites and all the sons of the east were lying in the valley as numerous as locusts; and their camels were without number, as numerous as the sand on the seashore. When Gideon came, behold, a man was relating a dream to his friend. And he said, "Behold, I had a dream; a loaf of barley bread was tumbling into the camp of Midian, and it came to the tent and struck it so that it fell, and turned it upside down so that the tent lay flat." His friend replied, "This is nothing less than the sword of Gideon the son of Joash, a man of Israel;

God has given Midian and all the camp into his hand."
When Gideon heard the account of the dream and its
interpretation, he bowed in worship. He returned to the
camp of Israel and said, "Arise, for the LORD has
given the camp of Midian into your hands."

He divided the 300 men into three companies,
and he put trumpets and empty pitchers into the hands
of all of them, with torches inside the pitchers. He said
to them, "Look at me and do likewise. And behold,
when I come to the outskirts of the camp, do as I do.
"When I and all who are with me blow the trumpet,
then you also blow the trumpets all around the camp
and say, 'For the LORD and for Gideon.'"

Gideon's army with torches and trumpets
Standard Bible Story Readers, Book Four -
Found on lavistachurchofchrist.org[54]

So Gideon and the hundred men who were
with him came to the outskirts of the camp at the
beginning of the middle watch, when they had just
posted the watch; and they blew the trumpets and
smashed the pitchers that were in their hands. When
the three companies blew the trumpets and broke the

pitchers, they held the torches in their left hands and
the trumpets in their right hands for blowing, and cried,
"A sword for the LORD and for Gideon!" Each stood
in his place around the camp; and all the army ran,
crying out as they fled. When they blew 300 trumpets,
the LORD set the sword of one against another even
throughout the whole army; and the army fled as far as
Beth-shittah toward Zererah, as far as the edge of Abel-
meholah, by Tabbath.

    The men of Israel were summoned from
Naphtali and Asher and all Manasseh, and they pursued
Midian. Gideon sent messengers throughout all the hill
country of Ephraim, saying, "Come down against
Midian and take the waters before them, as far as Beth-
barah and the Jordan."

    So all the men of Ephraim were summoned and
they took the waters as far as Beth-barah and the
Jordan. They captured the two leaders of Midian, Oreb
and Zeeb, and they killed Oreb at the rock of Oreb,
and they killed Zeeb at the wine press of Zeeb, while
they pursued Midian; and they brought the heads of
Oreb and Zeeb to Gideon from across the Jordan.

    Then the men of Ephraim said to him, "What is
this thing you have done to us, not calling us when you
went to fight against Midian?" And they contended
with him vigorously.

Have you even seen this before? Someone who did nothing
about a problem being indignant and trying to steal the glory after the
hard part is all over? Talk really is cheap, and it's easy to talk big after
everything is done.

    But he said to them, "What have I done now in
comparison with you? Is not the gleaning of the grapes
of Ephraim better than the vintage of Abiezer?

I'm not sure what this is. Gideon said that the left over grapes
of the men that didn't fight were better than the good grapes of his

family. Sounds like sucking up or something. I'm not sure. I think politicians today call that diplomacy, not sure. But I think a proverb states that a kind word deflects wrath or something like that, and Gideon didn't let pride get in the way (like I might have).

"God has given the leaders of Midian, Oreb and Zeeb into your hands; and what was I able to do in comparison with you?" Then their anger toward him subsided when he said that.

Then Gideon and the 300 men who were with him came to the Jordan and crossed over, weary yet pursuing. He said to the men of Succoth, "Please give loaves of bread to the people who are following me, for they are weary, and I am pursuing Zebah and Zalmunna, the kings of Midian." The leaders of Succoth said, "Are the hands of Zebah and Zalmunna already in your hands, that we should give bread to your army?" Gideon said, "All right, when the LORD has given Zebah and Zalmunna into my hand, then I will thrash your bodies with the thorns of the wilderness and with briers."

He went up from there to Penuel and spoke similarly to them; and the men of Penuel answered him just as the men of Succoth had answered. So he spoke also to the men of Penuel, saying, "When I return safely, I will tear down this tower."

Now Zebah and Zalmunna were in Karkor, and their armies with them, about 15,000 men, all who were left of the entire army of the sons of the east; for the fallen were 120,000 swordsmen. Gideon went up by the way of those who lived in tents on the east of Nobah and Jogbehah, and attacked the camp when the camp was unsuspecting. When Zebah and Zalmunna fled, he pursued them and captured the two kings of Midian, Zebah and Zalmunna, and routed the whole army. Then Gideon the son of Joash returned from the battle by the ascent of Heres. And he captured a youth from Succoth and questioned him.

Then the youth wrote down for him the princes of Succoth and its elders, seventy-seven men.

He came to the men of Succoth and said, "Behold Zebah and Zalmunna, concerning whom you taunted me, saying, 'Are the hands of Zebah and Zalmunna already in your hand, that we should give bread to your men who are weary?'" He took the elders of the city, and thorns of the wilderness and briers, and he disciplined the men of Succoth with them. He tore down the tower of Penuel and killed the men of the city.

Then he said to Zebah and Zalmunna, "What kind of men were they whom you killed at Tabor?" And they said, "They were like you, each one resembling the son of a king." He said, "They were my brothers, the sons of my mother. As the LORD lives, if only you had let them live, I would not kill you." So he said to Jether his firstborn, "Rise, kill them." But the youth did not draw his sword, for he was afraid, because he was still a youth. Then Zebah and Zalmunna said, "Rise up yourself, and fall on us; for as the man, so is his strength." So Gideon arose and killed Zebah and Zalmunna, and took the crescent ornaments which were on their camels' necks.

Jüdischer Oberpriester.   Leviten.

Jewish high priest wearing a hoshen, and
Levites in ancient Judah.
Author: THE HISTORY OF COSTUME By
Braun & Schneider
(Courtesy Wikipedia/Wikimedia)[55]

Then the men of Israel said to Gideon, "Rule
over us, both you and your son, also your son's son, for
you have delivered us from the hand of Midian." But
Gideon said to them, "I will not rule over you, nor shall
my son rule over you; the LORD shall rule over you."
Yet Gideon said to them, "I would request of
you, that each of you give me an earring from his
spoil." (For they had gold earrings, because they were
Ishmaelites.) They said, "We will surely give them." So
they spread out a garment, and every one of them

threw an earring there from his spoil. The weight of the gold earrings that he requested was 1,700 shekels of gold, besides the crescent ornaments and the pendants and the purple robes which were on the kings of Midian, and besides the neck bands that were on their camels' necks. Gideon made it into an ephod, and placed it in his city, Ophrah, and all Israel played the harlot with it there, so that it became a snare to Gideon and his household.

For more about Gideon, read Judges 6-7-8.

Tale #12
Life After Death

as told by

"The Ol' Turkey Hunter"

Shown below with a volunteer at a presentation of "The Parable of the Turkey Hunter". Volunteers are a big part of the program.

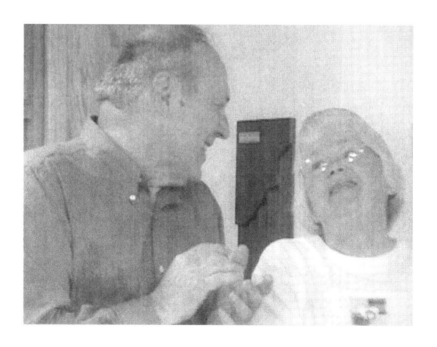

The Ol' Turkey Hunter

Life After Death

After Katie and I got married, I got into the habit of hunting instead of going to church on Sunday morning. Katie took the kids to church every Sunday morning and Sunday evening, and most Wednesday evenings; as I adopted the C & E plan. Christmas and Easter.

An unbelievable turn of events created a home Bible study group that replaced our church. Earlier, I talked about a boy at the boys' school who was hurt by "church people". Well, I found that some of the worst hurts you can get are hurts that are caused by our biological family members and our "church family". I guess the reason these hurts cut so deep is because these are the people that you so badly want to respect you and they are the people that you feel safe with.

The reason the Bible study group became our church is kind of complicated. Katie was very active in the church and taught a Sunday School class for youth. Katie has a gift from God relating to her ability to work with people. It's taken 38 years, but she has turned me from a red-necked heathen into a somewhat acceptable hillbilly. She has been a Family Advocate with Head Start for 20 years, working with 4-year-olds and their parents, isn't supervisor because she likes her summers off, and just has an unequaled way with people. Well, she got a letter from the preacher stating that because she was not faithful to the church, she could no longer be a Sunday School teacher. WHAT??? We were stunned. No questions, no warning, just out of the clear blue comes this letter.

Katie went to Sunday School and Church every Sunday and usually attended the Wednesday night service and tithed every week. The "pastor" cited that she had missed a few Wednesday night services and was thus not worthy of a position of leadership. Another excellent, extremely devoted and talented Sunday School teacher also received the letter. The church was so small anyway, maybe 30 people. Oh, well, you know when you are not wanted and we didn't let the door hit us in the butt.

It's interesting what happens to people when they get a little bit of power. Or maybe nothing happens, maybe they just get the chance to show their true colors. This particular preacher, after splitting our church, went to another church, split it up, and then got out of the business.

I think some people become preachers because they can't find a job anywhere else. Nobody will hire them or they don't want to work, so they say that they "hear a word from God" and VOILÀ, they are a preacher.

The group that was split from the church started a home Bible study group, 10 to 15 people, and eventually Katie hosted the study at our house. Of course, when the group meets at your house, you sit in on it, and as soon as I did, I was hooked. I learned a lot about everything as we studied the Bible. It was an awesome group of strong believers who became really good friends. They say that God works in mysterious ways.

The Bible studies were extremely interesting, but to make it even better, it became a social event. It always involved good food, and in the summer, we played sand volleyball on a court we built at our house, actually we built two courts.

People in our community knew of our group and if anyone had a problem, sickness or otherwise, they would call members of our Bible study for prayer.

It was a nice warm Sunday evening of volleyball before the food and the study. My friend, Dave, and his wife and their teenage son were all three on one team that night. On one play, Dave jumped for a block and his son jumped up as his dad was coming down and the son's knee hit his dad in the ribs. There was an audible bang or pop or snap or something, and the dad went down in the sand and didn't move. He was totally non-responsive.

Connie, that I have mentioned earlier, called everyone around to lay hands on him and pray. Well, you can see how strong my faith is because I went into the house and called the ambulance while everyone else prayed and laid hands on him. We were only a block from the fire house, so I walked up to meet the volunteer EMT's.

Beach Volleyball Spanish Championship 2004 in Laredo (Cantabria) (Courtesy Wikipedia/Wikimedia)[56]

My wife Katie stayed at Dave's side with the rest of the group. She has lots of experience with livestock and she later told me that he was making a "death rattle". That's an unconscious gurgling just before death.

The paramedics came and loaded him up. The hospital was about 30 miles away. Ten miles from the hospital, the EMT's lost his vital signs and pulled over until they could stabilize him.

Several of us followed him to the emergency room, sweaty and dirty and smelly. We were obviously very concerned and worried. The son was crying because he killed his dad. Mom was extremely upset, fearing the worst.

After a couple of hours, the doctor came out and said that he was sending Dave home, but he didn't have a shirt to wear, as it was now well after midnight and pretty cool outside. I gave the doctor my T-shirt, it was plenty big. However, the doctor brought the shirt back to the waiting room and said he wouldn't wear it because it was a Cubs T-shirt. We all knew that he was OK after that. The next thing we knew, we looked up at the window in the waiting room door and there was Dave with his nose and lips smashed up against the glass. How could he be dead two hours ago and now was making faces at us through the window? He was dead, flat lined in the ambulance and was now clowning around, no broken bones or punctured lungs, just a little sore. There's only one way that I can explain it. A miracle.

But if he was dead and came back to life, it wasn't the first time that it ever happened. Let's see what this bizarre story says.

> Now a certain man was sick, Lazarus of Bethany, the village of Mary and her sister Martha. It was the Mary who anointed the Lord with ointment, and wiped His feet with her hair, whose brother Lazarus was sick. So the sisters sent word to Him, saying, "Lord, behold, he whom You love is sick."
>
> But when Jesus heard this, He said, "This sickness is not to end in death, but for the glory of God, so that the Son of God may be glorified by it."
>
> Now Jesus loved Martha and her sister and Lazarus. So when He heard that he was sick, He then stayed two days longer in the place where He was. Then after this He said to the disciples, "Let us go to Judea again." The disciples said to Him, "Rabbi, the Jews were just now seeking to stone You, and are You going there again?"
>
> Jesus answered, "Are there not twelve hours in the day? If anyone walks in the day, he does not stumble, because he sees the light of this world. "But if anyone walks in the night, he stumbles, because the light is not in him." This He said, and after that He said to them, "Our friend Lazarus has fallen asleep; but I go, so that I may awaken him out of sleep."
>
> The disciples then said to Him, "Lord, if he has fallen asleep, he will recover." Now Jesus had spoken of his death, but they thought that He was speaking of literal sleep. So Jesus then said to them plainly, "Lazarus is dead, and I am glad for your sakes that I was not there, so that you may believe; but let us go to him."

Tomb of Saint Lazarus in Bethany Photo by Marion Doss
This file is licensed under the Creative Commons
Attribution ShareAlike 2.0 License.
(Courtesy Wikipedia/Wikimedia)[57]

Therefore Thomas, who is called Didymus, said to his fellow disciples, "Let us also go, so that we may die with Him."

So when Jesus came, He found that he had already been in the tomb four days. Now Bethany was near Jerusalem, about two miles off; and many of the Jews had come to Martha and Mary, to console them concerning their brother. Martha therefore, when she heard that Jesus was coming, went to meet Him, but Mary stayed at the house. Martha then said to Jesus, "Lord, if You had been here, my brother would not have died. Even now I know that whatever You ask of God, God will give You."

Jesus said to her, "Your brother will rise again." Martha said to Him, "I know that he will rise again in the resurrection on the last day." Jesus said to her, "I am the resurrection and the life; he who believes in Me will live even if he dies, and everyone who lives and believes in Me will never die. Do you believe this?"

She said to Him, "Yes, Lord; I have believed that You are the Christ, the Son of God, even He who comes into the world." When she had said this, she went away and called Mary her sister, saying secretly, "The Teacher is here and is calling for you." And when she heard it, she got up quickly and was coming to Him. Now Jesus had not yet come into the village, but was still in the place where Martha met Him. Then the Jews who were with her in the house, and consoling her, when they saw that Mary got up quickly and went out, they followed her, supposing that she was going to the tomb to weep there.

Therefore, when Mary came where Jesus was, she saw Him, and fell at His feet, saying to Him, "Lord, if You had been here, my brother would not have died." When Jesus therefore saw her weeping, and the Jews who came with her also weeping, He was deeply moved in spirit and was troubled, and said, "Where have you laid him?" They said to Him, "Lord, come and see."

Jesus wept. **(The shortest verse in the Bible).**
So the Jews were saying, "See how He loved him!" But some of them said, "Could not this man, who opened the eyes of the blind man, have kept this man also from dying?" So Jesus, again being deeply moved within, came to the tomb. Now it was a cave, and a stone was lying against it.

Jesus said, "Remove the stone." Martha, the sister of the deceased, said to Him, "Lord, by this time there will be a stench, for he has been dead four days." Jesus said to her, "Did I not say to you that if you believe, you will see the glory of God?" So they removed the stone. Then Jesus raised His eyes, and said, "Father, I thank You that You have heard Me. "I knew that You always hear Me; but because of the people standing around I said it, so that they may believe that You sent Me."

Vincent Van Gogh: La Résurrection de Lazare (d'après Rembrandt)/
The Raising of Lazarus (after Rembrandt) (1889-1890)
(Courtesy Wikipedia/Wikimedia)[58]

THE RAISING CИ LAZARIS.
Late 14th — early 15th Century. Byzantium From the
Collection of G. Gamon-Gumun. Russian museum
(Courtesy Wikipedia/Wikimedia)[59]

When He had said these things, He cried out
with a loud voice, "Lazarus, come forth." The man who

had died came forth, bound hand and foot with wrappings, and his face was wrapped around with a cloth. Jesus said to them, "Unbind him, and let him go."

Therefore many of the Jews who came to Mary, and saw what He had done, believed in Him. But some of them went to the Pharisees and told them the things which Jesus had done.

For more on this story, read John 11.

Tale #13
The Ten Suggestions

as told by

"The Ol' Turkey Hunter"

Shown here with the Red Sox. Most turkey hunters like to coach sports in the off season.

The Ol' Turkey Hunter

The Ten Suggestions

Famine had forced Abraham's grandson, Jacob, and Jacob's twelve sons out of the promised land of Canaan into Egypt for food to survive. Jacob's family found favor from Pharaoh (that's a long story that we won't go into now) and was granted a place to live in the rich delta area of the Nile River, an area called Goshen. I always wondered what an old neighbor was talking about when she said "Land o' Goshen". Well, that's kind of like the Garden of Eden or "it don't get much better than this".

God had promised Abraham that his decedents would be as numerous as the stars in the heavens, and they multiplied greatly while in Egypt. It got to the point where the new Pharaoh, who never knew Jacob because Jacob had lived 400 years prior to this, became afraid of the sheer numbers of Israelites, and subjected them to very harsh slavery. But the Israelites just kept multiplying like rabbits, so finally the king became so afraid and so desperate that he ordered the midwives to kill all of the male Hebrew babies. (I think Jews, Hebrews, and Israelites are all names for the same people.) But unlike the doctors in the United States today, they could not kill a newborn baby. Probably didn't get enough money for it.

Israel in Egypt by Edward Poynter
(Courtesy Wikipedia/Wikimedia)[60]

Since that didn't work for Pharaoh, he ordered his soldiers to throw all male children of the Israelites into the Nile River to kill them.

191

This kind of goes back to my "one extreme follows another" theory. It was about the time Moses was born that they fed the babies to the crocodiles. Moses was the person that led the Israelites out of Egypt, through the desert and to the doorstep of the promised land.

Peter Paul Rubens' painting, Massacre of the Innocents.
1611 or 1612

I wanted a picture here of the Egyptians throwing the Hebrew babies into the Nile River to be eaten by crocodiles, but I couldn't find one. Instead I found this painting where all of the Hebrew males under 2 years of age were slaughtered at the order of King Herod about 1 AD after the wise men told him that they were going to see the newborn king. I know the killing of infants has to be extremely horrific, but I don't know hy the old painters always had to have naked men doing the killing.

(Courtesy Wikipedia/Wikimedia)[61]

While the Israelites were wandering around in the desert, this is where we get to the "Ten Suggestions". I just love Zig Ziglar. I've listened to his tapes and spent hours reading his books, and my wife,

192

Katie, and I even spent $50 a piece to go to one of his seminars in St. Louis about 15 years ago. He's just awesome.

One of his talking points is about the "Ten Suggestions". He'd say, in that unique, slow, salesman drawl, "Now, you notice (pause for effect) they don't call it the (pause again) Ten Suggestions." No, they call it the Ten Commandments.

But you know what, I think maybe it really should be called the Ten Suggestions. God created man with a "free will" to make his own choices, and if we are commanded, I don't think we pay much attention to what we are commanded.

And the suggestions, if we follow the ten suggestions, it seems things go much better in our lives. Let's look at the story and I'll explain more later.

In the third month after the sons of Israel had gone out of the land of Egypt, on that very day they came into the wilderness of Sinai. When they set out from Rephidim, they came to the wilderness of Sinai and camped in the wilderness; and there Israel camped in front of the mountain.

Moses went up to God, and the LORD called to him from the mountain, saying, "Thus you shall say to the house of Jacob and tell the sons of Israel: 'You yourselves have seen what I did to the Egyptians, and how I bore you on eagles' wings, and brought you to Myself. Now then, if you will indeed obey My voice and keep My covenant, then you shall be My own possession among all the peoples, for all the earth is Mine; and you shall be to Me a kingdom of priests and a holy nation.' These are the words that you shall speak to the sons of Israel."

So Moses came and called the elders of the people, and set before them all these words which the LORD had commanded him.

All the people answered together and said, "All that the LORD has spoken we will do!" And Moses brought back the words of the people to the LORD.

The LORD said to Moses, "Behold, I will come to you in a thick cloud, so that the people may hear when I speak with you and may also believe in you forever." Then Moses told the words of the people to the LORD.

The LORD also said to Moses, "Go to the people and consecrate them today and tomorrow, and let them wash their garments; and let them be ready for the third day, for on the third day the LORD will come down on Mount Sinai in the sight of all the people. You shall set bounds for the people all around, saying, 'Beware that you do not go up on the mountain or touch the border of it; whoever touches the mountain shall surely be put to death. No hand shall touch him, but he shall surely be stoned or shot through; whether beast or man, he shall not live.' When the ram's horn sounds a long blast, they shall come up to the mountain."

So Moses went down from the mountain to the people and consecrated the people, and they washed their garments. He said to the people, "Be ready for the third day; do not go near a woman."

So it came about on the third day, when it was morning, that there were thunder and lightning flashes and a thick cloud upon the mountain and a very loud trumpet sound, so that all the people who were in the camp trembled. And Moses brought the people out of the camp to meet God, and they stood at the foot of the mountain. Now Mount Sinai was all in smoke because the LORD descended upon it in fire; and its smoke ascended like the smoke of a furnace, and the whole mountain quaked violently. When the sound of the trumpet grew louder and louder, Moses spoke and God answered him with thunder.

View from the summit of Mt. Sinai
(Courtesy Wikipedia/Wikimedia)[62]

The LORD came down on Mount Sinai, to the top of the mountain; and the LORD called Moses to the top of the mountain, and Moses went up. Then the LORD spoke to Moses, "Go down, warn the people, so that they do not break through to the LORD to gaze, and many of them perish. Also let the priests who come near to the LORD consecrate themselves, or else the LORD will break out against them." Moses said to the LORD, "The people cannot come up to Mount Sinai, for You warned us, saying, 'Set bounds about the mountain and consecrate it.'"

Then the LORD said to him, "Go down and come up again, you and Aaron with you; but do not let the priests and the people break through to come up to the LORD, or He will break forth upon them." So Moses went down to the people and told them.

Then God spoke all these words, saying, "I am the LORD your God, who brought you out of the land of Egypt, out of the house of slavery.

"You shall have no other gods before Me.

"You shall not make for yourself an idol, or any likeness of what is in heaven above or on the earth beneath or in the water under the earth.

"You shall not worship them or serve them; for I, the LORD your God, am a jealous God, visiting the iniquity of the fathers on the children, on the third and the fourth generations of those who hate Me, but showing lovingkindness to thousands, to those who love Me and keep My commandments.

10 commandments by Rembrandt
(Courtesy Wikipedia/Wikimedia)[63]

"You shall not take the name of the LORD
your God in vain, for the LORD will not leave him
unpunished who takes His name in vain.

"Remember the sabbath day, to keep it holy. Six
days you shall labor and do all your work, but the
seventh day is a sabbath of the LORD your God; in it
you shall not do any work, you or your son or your
daughter, your male or your female servant or your
cattle or your sojourner who stays with you. For in six
days the LORD made the heavens and the earth, the
sea and all that is in them, and rested on the seventh
day; therefore the LORD blessed the sabbath day and
made it holy.

"Honor your father and your mother, that your days may be prolonged in the land which the LORD your God gives you.

"You shall not murder.

"You shall not commit adultery.

"You shall not steal.

"You shall not bear false witness against your neighbor.

"You shall not covet your neighbor's house; you shall not covet your neighbor's wife or his male servant or his female servant or his ox or his donkey or anything that belongs to your neighbor."

All the people perceived the thunder and the lightning flashes and the sound of the trumpet and the mountain smoking; and when the people saw it, they trembled and stood at a distance. Then they said to Moses, "Speak to us yourself and we will listen; but let not God speak to us, or we will die."

Talk about the "fear of God". That reminds me of a story about a little bird that was freezing and kept trying to fly through a glass window pane to get warm. The man went outside to help the little bird, but it was scared of him, even though the man was just trying to help the little bird. The man was different and created fear in the bird, so the bird would not let the man help him. I think we are a lot the same in many ways.

Moses said to the people, "Do not be afraid; for God has come in order to test you, and in order that the fear of Him may remain with you, so that you may not sin."

Today if something like that happened, I'm not sure people would pay much attention. Oh, yeah, it would show up in the Enquirer and the Star, maybe Entertainment Tonight on TV, but with all of the special effects in the movies and on computers, I don't know what affect that would have on people today.

But back in the day, that had to be a tremendous shock. The world had never seen such a sight and sounds. It even says the people were terrified. God did this to impress upon his people that they need to follow these guidelines. FOR REAL!!! However, if you read the rest of the story, the Israelites have a shorter memory than I do, and that's pretty bad.

The place we, as a country, have fallen down is in passing our values on to the next generation. I think this has a lot to do with the media. Even though "Rock and Roll" was pretty radical with some of their lyrics, television was still pretty wholesome with shows like Timmy and Lassie, Dragnet, Andy Griffith, and the cartoons. I loved the cartoons. Foghorn Leghorn. Rocky and Bullwinkle, Yogi Bear and Boo-boo, El-kabong. I watched them all. At that time I don't think the Mickey Mouse Club had subliminal images of body parts or whatever like the Disney kid movies have today. And most of the cartoons today have nasty, pouty faced-kids being pissed off about something all of the time. I could go on and on about the terrible influences of TV and movies on our kids today. Although there are many wonderful kids today, I'm afraid that the effects of today's morality has already had a very detrimental effect on our youth as a whole and maybe even ruined the future of our country.

As I've mentioned before, I worked at the boys' school and we had Parent-Child Seminars where usually the young men had not seen their parents for several months. One segment of the seminar consisted of the parents and child working together to list their family values. Almost always, the list included honesty, respect, responsibility, love, all of those good things alluded to in the ten commandments.

For a long time, I wondered how the parents failed to transfer their values to their children. Then, like a bolt of lightning, I had a

"DUH" moment. They DID transfer their values to their children. About half of the boys came from homes with divorced parents and I've talked to enough divorced people to know that love, respect, etc. are not compatible with divorce no matter what they say. Often times divorced folks try to fool themselves and justify things by saying they get along well. WHAT!!!!!!! Maybe after the divorce and they are seldom if ever together, but definitely not before. I used to be a sucker and accept that, but we both know that's a bunch of B.S. Someone said that marriage is grand, but divorce is about 50 Grand. And that's conservative in many cases. Wounds from divorce are deep and never heal, NEVER.

And even parents that are not divorced, it's extremely difficult to raise a child today. At the boys' academy, I saw many parents that I think would have been better off getting a dog than a child. Of course there are great parents that sometimes have a child go astray, especially if they get in with the wrong group and get started on drugs. But even then there are sometimes underlying reasons that this happens.

I observed that, in an emergency situation like the academy, in a last ditch effort to save a child, parents resorted to the basic core values of the Bible. Back to the Bible. The program did not present itself as being Biblical, but it's concepts were straight from the Bible. Parents and children both found that the ten suggestions aren't a threat or punishment, they are the guidelines we need to follow for a fulfilling life.

I thought that sending a child to the academy was like sending an unruly dog to obedience school. Kids and dogs both do better when they have structure and discipline. Structure and discipline. Have you seen the super nanny shows? Structure and discipline with a little bit of time and love thrown in. Responses are almost immediate.

The Bible talks about sparing the rod and spoiling the child. Actually it says in Proverbs,

> He who withholds his rod hates his son, But he who loves him disciplines him diligently.

A rod may be extreme, but maybe not. When parents start out at a very early age, palm of hand on seat of pants works wonders. In my case, I only got one major adjustment from my mom and lots of minor adjustments from my dad. Dad was subtle. Like in church, when I became too distractive, the hand-clamp on my leg would get tighter and tighter until I got the message and stopped squirming. As I got older, it was the thump. Like a bolt of lightning out of the heavens, THUMP. The middle finger of the right hand building up pressure on the opposable thumb until the thumb releases the middle finger which flies forcefully forward, and THUMP, right on top of the head. I bet Dad was good at throwing spit wads in school because his timing was perfect. With Dad's THUMP method of correction, there was no big drama, no arguement, you just knew not to do it again. Dr. Spock probably wouldn't approve, but I believe that it was genious.

And then the major adjustment. One Sunday after church we were changing clothes, and I put my younger brother over the foot of the bed and he went squalling to Mom. Unfortunately for me, the nearest instructional tool available to her was a twisted wire fly swatter. I remember the plastic swatter on the end flew off leaving a twisted wire. Boy, twisted wire on whitey tighteys, man, that will get your attention.

But that can't happen today. Parents can't even swat their child on the seat anymore. Kate of Jon and Kate Plus Eight was caught on film swatting one of her children, appropriately on the seat, and the tabloids crucified her about it. I've heard of children being taken away from parents and parents placed in jail for disciplining their children. I bet John Wayne is raw from rolling over in his grave.

One discipline that I've learned from the boys' school is the discipline of an adoptive parent. If there is a natural parent, it is the natural parents' responsibility to discipline their biological child. Relationships are already too strained in a step-parent/step-child situation to add the extra resentment of discipline from someone who does not have the inherent authority of a natural parent and in most cases has not put in the time and effort to have earned that authority.

And remember what God said about *"visiting the iniquity of the fathers on the children, on the third and the fourth generations of those who hate Me,"*. Does that make sense? Sure. Same sex parents are the most influential person in a child's life. If dad has no regard for the values that most people consider important, what chance does the son have of developing a moral conscience?

So the people stood at a distance, while Moses approached the thick cloud where God was. Then the LORD said to Moses, "Thus you shall say to the sons of Israel, 'You yourselves have seen that I have spoken to you from heaven. You shall not make other gods besides Me; gods of silver or gods of gold, you shall not make for yourselves. You shall make an altar of earth for Me, and you shall sacrifice on it your burnt offerings and your peace offerings, your sheep and your oxen; in every place where I cause My name to be remembered, I will come to you and bless you. If you make an altar of stone for Me, you shall not build it of cut stones, for if you wield your tool on it, you will profane it. And you shall not go up by steps to My altar, so that your nakedness will not be exposed on it.'

There's a lot more to this story in the Book of Exodus.

The Ol' Turkey Hunter

Tale #14
Church Hurts

as told by

"The Ol' Turkey Hunter"

Shown here with Janet, DuWayne's wife, an honorary turkey hunter, with some of the blackberry jelly she made. Turkey hunters know where all of the good blackberries, raspberries, gooseberries, and wild plums are located. Last year was Janet's first year picking wild blackberries. After crossing a rusty old barb wire fence, stepping over a thorny locust tree trunk that had fallen over, swatting a mosquito on her hand, and pulling her sleeve away from a thorny briar, she said, "I can see that this is sport." This year she was a pro.

The Ol' Turkey Hunter

Church Hurts

I've never heard the audible voice of God. That's actually kind of a scary thought. Like a tornado. I'm a math and physics person. I was always fascinated by tornados and I always wanted to see one. I'd heard so many stories of cows up in trees and wheat straws blown into trees without breaking the straw. One of the most incredible forces of nature, incredible power, a tornado was on the top of my list of things to see.

Well, be careful what you wish for, I got my wish. When my son, Tim, was one year old, he and my wife, Katie, and Katie's niece, Laura Lee, were with me in the old Dodge on a gravel road in western Illinois when we made a right hand turn, and there it was. It was HUGE!!! And there was nowhere to run. So what do you do in a split second emergency? I hit the gas. 70 MPH on a gravel road trying to get around a tornado. Really stupid. I thought that it was like 100 yards away, but I drove a mile and a half before we got around it. It was south of us, heading northeast, and I was east of it going due west at 70 MPH trying to get around it.

After we got past it, the tornado hit the town of Plymouth a couple of miles away. One of Katie's best friends was running for cover with her 2 year old daughter when the wind lifted the baby out of her mother's arms and broke the baby's arm. Also, I saw a picture in the newspaper where a tree went down and ran a big limb through the hood and engine block of their Camaro. I don't remember, but I'm sure it totaled the car.

Tornado

This looks like the early stages of a tornado. New tornados are white like a cloud until they hit the ground and fill up with dirt. This one doesn't look nearly as big as the tornado we ran away from, but then I'm not 400 yards away from it, either.

(Courtesy Wikipedia/Wikimedia)[64]

Well, obviously we made it through the tornado because I'm still here to tell about it, but it was really scary. After that, whenever there was a tornado watch, we went straight to the nasty old basement of our farmhouse. Moved a TV and chairs to the basement just for tornado watches. For 30 years now, I have dreamed about getting away and hiding from tornados. It seems so real when you are asleep and dreaming.

But my point here is that something that seems so exciting or unique may have unexpected ramifications and responsibilities.

I mentioned that I have never heard the audible voice of God, but I have a friend who claims that he did when he was just a child. He has been a Pentecostal preacher for many years, and I must say, he is an excellent pastor.

So let's see what happened to Samuel, the last judge of Israel before the Hebrews demanded a king, a monarchy-type government like the inhabitants of Canaan.

Now there was a certain man from Ramathaim-zophim from the hill country of Ephraim, and his name was Elkanah the son of Jeroham, the son of Elihu, the son of Tohu, the son of Zuph, an Ephraimite. He had two wives: the name of one was Hannah and the name of the other Peninnah; and Peninnah had children, but Hannah had no children.

Now this man would go up from his city yearly to worship and to sacrifice to the LORD of hosts in Shiloh. And the two sons of Eli, Hophni and Phinehas, were priests to the LORD there. When the day came that Elkanah sacrificed, he would give portions to Peninnah his wife and to all her sons and her daughters; but to Hannah he would give a double portion, for he loved Hannah, but the LORD had closed her womb.

It was a really big disgrace and considered a curse for women who did not have children.

Her rival, however, would provoke her bitterly to irritate her, because the LORD had closed her womb. It happened year after year, as often as she went up to the house of the LORD, she would provoke her; so she wept and would not eat. Then Elkanah her husband said to her, "Hannah, why do you weep and why do you not eat and why is your heart sad? Am I not better to you than ten sons?"

Then Hannah rose after eating and drinking in Shiloh. Now Eli the priest was sitting on the seat by the doorpost of the temple of the LORD. She, greatly distressed, prayed to the LORD and wept bitterly. She made a vow and said, "O LORD of hosts, if You will indeed look on the affliction of Your maidservant and remember me, and not forget Your maidservant, but will give Your maidservant a son, then I will give him to the LORD all the days of his life, and a razor shall never come on his head."

Now it came about, as she continued praying before the LORD, that Eli was watching her mouth. As for Hannah, she was speaking in her heart, only her lips were moving, but her voice was not heard. So Eli thought she was drunk. Then Eli said to her, "How long will you make yourself drunk? Put away your wine from you."

But Hannah replied, "No, my lord, I am a woman oppressed in spirit; I have drunk neither wine nor strong drink, but I have poured out my soul before the LORD. Do not consider your maidservant as a worthless woman, for I have spoken until now out of my great concern and provocation."

Then Eli answered and said, "Go in peace; and may the God of Israel grant your petition that you have asked of Him."

She said, "Let your maidservant find favor in your sight." So the woman went her way and ate, and her face was no longer sad.

Then they arose early in the morning and worshiped before the LORD, and returned again to their house in Ramah.

And Elkanah had relations with Hannah his wife, and the LORD remembered her. It came about in due time, after Hannah had conceived, that she gave birth to a son; and she named him Samuel, saying, "Because I have asked him of the LORD."

She said, "Oh, my lord! As your soul lives, my lord, I am the woman who stood here beside you, praying to the LORD. "For this boy I prayed, and the LORD has given me my petition which I asked of Him. So I have also dedicated him to the LORD; as long as he lives he is dedicated to the LORD." And he worshiped the LORD there.

Infant Samuel by Joshua Reynolds 1723
(Courtesy Wikipedia/Wikimedia)[65]

Then the man Elkanah went up with all his
household to offer to the LORD the yearly sacrifice
and pay his vow. But Hannah did not go up, for she
said to her husband, "I will not go up until the child is
weaned; then I will bring him, that he may appear
before the LORD and stay there forever."

Elkanah her husband said to her, "Do what
seems best to you. Remain until you have weaned him;
only may the LORD confirm His word." So the woman
remained and nursed her son until she weaned him.

Now when she had weaned him, she took him
up with her, with a three-year-old bull and one ephah
of flour and a jug of wine, and brought him to the
house of the LORD in Shiloh, although the child was
young. Then they slaughtered the bull, and brought the
boy to Eli.

Anna presenting her son Samuel to the priest Eli
ca. 1665
Gerbrand van den Eeckhout (1621–1674)
(Courtesy Wikipedia/Wikimedia)[66]

I'm not a Bible scholar, but I think Samuel was
considered a nazarite. That is a person who has been dedicated
to God and promises not to cut their hair or drink wine.
Sampson was another nazarite. Sampson lost his superhuman
strength when he broke his mother's vow that he would never
cut his hair.

Some time later as Samuel was growing up:

> Now Samuel was ministering before the
> LORD, as a boy wearing a linen ephod. And his
> mother would make him a little robe and bring it to
> him from year to year when she would come up with
> her husband to offer the yearly sacrifice. Then Eli
> would bless Elkanah and his wife and say, "May the
> LORD give you children from this woman in place of
> the one she dedicated to the LORD." And they went to
> their own home.

The LORD visited Hannah; and she conceived and gave birth to three sons and two daughters and the boy Samuel grew before the LORD.

Now the boy Samuel was ministering to the LORD before Eli and word from the LORD was rare in those days, visions were infrequent. It happened at that time as Eli was lying down in his place (now his eyesight had begun to grow dim and he could not see well), and the lamp of God had not yet gone out, and Samuel was lying down in the temple of the LORD where the ark of God was, that the LORD called Samuel; and he said, "Here I am."

Then he ran to Eli and said, "Here I am, for you called me." But he said, "I did not call, lie down again." So he went and lay down. The LORD called yet again, "Samuel!" So Samuel arose and went to Eli and said, "Here I am, for you called me." But he answered, "I did not call, my son, lie down again."

Now Samuel did not yet know the LORD, nor had the word of the LORD yet been revealed to him. So the LORD called Samuel again for the third time. And he arose and went to Eli and said, "Here I am, for you called me." Then Eli discerned that the LORD was calling the boy.

And Eli said to Samuel, "Go lie down, and it shall be if He calls you, that you shall say, 'Speak, LORD, for Your servant is listening.'"

So Samuel went and lay down in his place. Then the LORD came and stood and called as at other times, "Samuel! Samuel!" And Samuel said, "Speak, for Your servant is listening."

The LORD said to Samuel, "Behold, I am about to do a thing in Israel at which both ears of everyone who hears it will tingle. In that day I will carry out against Eli all that I have spoken concerning his house, from beginning to end.

Eli was the high priest of Israel, but he had two sons (sounds like some preachers kids I've known) who were out of control and caused lots of trouble. You can read more about that in 1 Samuel 2.

"For I have told him that I am about to judge
his house forever for the iniquity which he knew,
because his sons brought a curse on themselves and he
did not rebuke them. Therefore I have sworn to the
house of Eli that the iniquity of Eli's house shall not be
atoned for by sacrifice or offering forever." So Samuel
lay down until morning. Then he opened the doors of
the house of the LORD. But Samuel was afraid to tell
the vision to Eli.
Then Eli called Samuel and said, "Samuel, my
son." And he said, "Here I am." He said, "What is the
word that He spoke to you? Please do not hide it from
me. May God do so to you, and more also, if you hide
anything from me of all the words that He spoke to
you." So Samuel told him everything and hid nothing
from him. And he said, "It is the LORD; let Him do
what seems good to Him."
Thus Samuel grew and the LORD was with
him and let none of his words fail. All Israel from Dan
even to Beersheba knew that Samuel was confirmed as
a prophet of the LORD.

Having been consecrated to God, I'm sure Samuel had thought about talking to God, but I don't think he expected to hear audibly. And like I mentioned earlier, sometimes there are lots of responsibilities associated with something special like that. And in Samuel's case, to have to pronounce a curse on your mentor and the Chief Priest, not a fun position to be in.

But does God only speak to humans in an audible voice? Over the last couple of years I believe that God has communicated to me in two different methods, giving me scriptures and giving me ideas, usually in the middle of the night. Let me explain.

I present a program I call The Parable of the Turkey Hunter, thus the pen name The Ol' Turkey Hunter. It includes all types of turkey calls, owl calls, crow calls, decoys, and camouflage. For nursing home residents, it addresses loneliness and discouragement. At the end of the program, I shake hands with every person who attends and try to speak briefly with each one. At Quincy, a little old lady in a wheel chair hung on to my hand. She told me that she was a handwriting analyst, and asked me where I got this presentation. I said I didn't know. But she persisted, "You had to get it somewhere." I shrugged my shoulders and replied, "I guess God gave it to me, I don' know." So if God did give it to me, I think I need to be sharing it with others.

So in order to get the chance to speak to more people, I went to Quincy, IL at WTJR TV (Working Till Jesus Returns) to talk to Dr. Debra Peppers, National Teacher of the Year and radio talk show host, to get some ideas. She suggested that I write my book. Write my book? What book?

After several days, it occurred to me that the book wasn't about me. It was about the stories that I like to tell. Now it seems that this book is the natural conclusion of many bizarre things that have happened to me in my lifetime. In Romans 8:28, it says, *"And we know that all things work together for good to them that love God."* Boy, there have been a lot of things in my life that I didn't understand why at the time, and many of them I REALLY, REALLY didn't enjoy. In fact, two or three incidents were totally devastating at the time. So writing this book at age 57 could make the first 56 years of my life make a little bit more sense, if that's what I'm supposed to do. If this book is not for a purpose, I'm totally lost.

My purpose?!. My purpose in writing this book is four-fold. One, to be entertaining. Two, to educate folks about some of the things in the Bible. Three, to create interest in reading the Bible. And fourth, to help people understand more about themselves and the situations they find themselves in during their lives.

The first way I think God has communicated with me is by putting ideas in my head. People who know me know that I'm pretty random at times. I don't know where these ideas come from. I haven't experienced any dreams or visions, but many, many times I wake up at 2:30 am with ideas rolling around in my head. Then I lay in bed and spend a couple of hours thinking things through. These ideas just seem to come "out of the blue". I usually have to take two Tylenol PM's if I want to sleep through the night. That's one place I get some material for this book and I don't know why.

The second way I think God communicates with me is through Bible verses. For some reason, it seems that when I'm really confused and upset and really, really need guidance, when I randomly open the Bible, the Book falls opens to a verse or chapter that fits my situation perfectly and gives me much needed insight, peace, and direction.

So now I'm finally getting to the title of this short story. Church Hurts. The name doesn't really apply to the story of Samuel. I've "beat around the bush" to get to what's really on my mind, church hurts. I've experienced them myself, and I've seen many other people who have been severely wounded by other church people.

I've found that some of our most painful emotional injuries are inflicted by close family members and close church friends. They are the people that mean the most to us and we feel safe with them in that we don't expect them to abandon us or attack us. This may just be me trying to "vent" my frustration or me "whining" about how I was "wronged", but here goes.

I was a board member at our church when, to make a long, ugly story short, the pastor lied to his board members to save his job, illegally took over the church's checking account, and revoked the church membership of lifetime members and refused to let them vote at the annual meeting. The membership appealed to the district, who stood behind the "so-called" pastor. I could not believe that the district would stand behind the criminal activity of any preacher, but they did.

I was livid. At the appeals hearing with the district, I was about to explode when, in front of 10-15 people, I screamed out to God to help me. Instantly I experienced the "peace that passes understanding". I was like a balloon that was filled so tightly that it was ready to burst, and instantly, I became as limp as a dishrag. I just can't describe the extremes of emotion in a matter of 1 second.

However, I was still extremely troubled that night and couldn't sleep, feeling that I had let down so many of the other members of the congregation, so about 1:00 am I opened up the Bible. I just flopped it open and there was Psalm 109. I was amazed when I read that chapter, it described my situation perfectly. Here is Psalm 109.

O God of my praise,
Do not be silent!
For they have opened the wicked and deceitful mouth

against me;
They have spoken against me with a lying tongue.
They have also surrounded me with words of hatred,
And fought against me without cause.
In return for my love they act as my accusers;
But I am in prayer.
Thus they have repaid me evil for good
And hatred for my love.

I've been married for 38 years and have never experienced divorce, but I suspect that a lot of divorced people feel the same way about their relationship with their ex-spouse.

Appoint a wicked man over him,
And let an accuser stand at his right hand.
When he is judged, let him come forth guilty,
And let his prayer become sin.
Let his days be few;
Let another take his office.
Let his children be fatherless
And his wife a widow.
Let his children wander about and beg;
And let them seek sustenance far from their ruined homes.
Let the creditor seize all that he has,
And let strangers plunder the product of his labor.
Let there be none to extend lovingkindness to him,
Nor any to be gracious to his fatherless children.
Let his posterity be cut off;
In a following generation let their name be blotted out.
Let the iniquity of his fathers be remembered before the LORD,
And do not let the sin of his mother be blotted out.
Let them be before the LORD continually,
That He may cut off their memory from the earth;
Because he did not remember to show lovingkindness,

But persecuted the afflicted and needy man,
And the despondent in heart, to put them to death.
He also loved cursing, so it came to him;
And he did not delight in blessing, so it was far from him.
But he clothed himself with cursing as with his garment,
And it entered into his body like water
And like oil into his bones.
Let it be to him as a garment with which he covers himself,
And for a belt with which he constantly girds himself.
Let this be the reward of my accusers from the LORD,
And of those who speak evil against my soul.
But You, O GOD, the Lord, deal kindly with me for Your name's sake;
Because Your lovingkindness is good, deliver me;
For I am afflicted and needy,
And my heart is wounded within me.
I am passing like a shadow when it lengthens;
I am shaken off like the locust.
My knees are weak from fasting,
And my flesh has grown lean, without fatness.
I also have become a reproach to them;
When they see me, they wag their head.
Help me, O LORD my God;
Save me according to Your lovingkindness.
And let them know that this is Your hand;
You, LORD, have done it.
Let them curse, but You bless;
When they arise, they shall be ashamed,
But Your servant shall be glad.
Let my accusers be clothed with dishonor,
And let them cover themselves with their own shame as with a robe.
With my mouth I will give thanks abundantly to the LORD;
And in the midst of many I will praise Him.

For He stands at the right hand of the needy,
To save him from those who judge his soul.

I have no ill-will toward this man's children, and I have tried very hard to forgive this man, but I really felt that God had opened the book to this particular verse to help me deal with the situation. I was going crazy.

King of all Israel and Judah
Attribution: José-Manuel Benito Álvarez
(Courtesy Wikipedia/Wikimedia)[67]

These were the words of David, I'm not sure if it was before or after he became king of Israel, but he was the anointed of God and except for one bad screw-up, a very good example of someone after God's own heart. After reading the chapter twice, I went to bed and slept like a baby. There have been other times when I've popped the Bible open and the first verse I read seems to apply directly to my situation, but this example is a "no doubter" to me.

Maybe I shouldn't have included this little bit of personal smut, but I think that many people have experienced "church hurts". They come in all shapes and sizes, but they all do damage.

And church hurts work both ways. I recently talked to a man who preached for 10 years. He said that it was the most rewarding job he ever had, but that it was also the most devastating job that he ever had. I figure the devastating part is why he is no longer in the pulpit.

You know, it seems that beer is a great uniter. I used to watch "Cheers" on TV. It was a great group of friends from all walks of life. It seemed that they were not as critical of each other as church people, or if they were, it was meant in a more constructive or helpful way, and not as being so judgmental. Maybe we can learn an important lesson from the local pub.

I once heard my pastor preach on the "salt of the earth". He suggested that maybe church-goers should be like salt; sprinkled sparingly to season things instead of being dumped in a pile to "suck the water out of a situation".

It sometimes seems that a "born again" Christian is a lot like a recovering alcoholic. Both tend to be overly judgmental and present their message in a way that nobody wants to be around either of them. It's not our job to convict, that's the Holy Spirits job.

Anyway, to wind this up, there are several places in the Bible where people have heard the audible voice of God. See how many you can find.

Tale #15

The Promised Land

as told by

"The Ol' Turkey Hunter"

Shown here with Nathan and two limits of pheasants in Iowa, a little piece of God's country.

The Ol' Turkey Hunter

.

The Promised Land

A merica, the great melting pot. There is an inscription in the Statue of Liberty that is an excerpt from a poem by Emma Lazarus.

The statue as viewed from the ground on Liberty Island
(Courtesy Wikipedia/Wikimedia)[68]

The figure in Jules Joseph Lefebvre's painting *La Vérité* - produced in 1870, the same year as the first model of the Statue of Liberty - strikes a similar pose to that of the statue (Musée d'Orsay, Paris) (Courtesy Wikipedia/Wikimedia)[69]

First Lady Nancy Reagan waves from the Statue of Liberty after she re opened the structure on its 100th birthday (Courtesy Wikipedia/Wikimedia)[70]

The name of the poem is "The New Colossus". I'm not sure if the New Colossus is the Statue of Liberty or the United States itself, but the poem goes like this:

The New Colossus

by Emma Lazarus

Not like the brazen giant of Greek fame,
with conquering limbs astride from land to land;
Here at our sea-washed, sunset gates shall stand
a mighty woman with a torch, whose flame
is the imprisoned lightning, and her name
Mother of Exiles. From her beacon-hand
glows world-wide welcome; her mild eyes command
the air-bridged harbor that twin cities frame.
"Keep ancient lands, your storied pomp!" cries she
with silent lips. "Give me your tired, your poor,
your huddled masses yearning to breathe free,
the wretched refuse of your teeming shore.
Send these, the homeless, tempest-tost to me,
I lift my lamp beside the golden door!" [2]

I see a big similarity between the development of Americans and Jewish people. Abraham, father of the Jews, was chosen by God to be his people. When America was born, Americans chose the God of Abraham to be their God.

Abraham had to leave his family homeland and make a new start in a strange, foreign land. Immigrants left their homelands and took a scary, but hope-filled trip across the Atlantic Ocean to arrive at Ellis Island. Abraham took a step of faith and obedience; Americans-to-be took a step of faith and hope.

Immigrants with their first look at their "Promised Land"
Jewish Women's Archive. "JWA - Emma Lazarus - The New
Colossus." (October 8, 2009).[71]

Now the LORD said to Abram, [*God later
changed the name Abram to Abraham*]
Go forth from your country,
And from your relatives
And from your father's house,
To the land which I will show you;
And I will make you a great nation,
And I will bless you,
And make your name great;
And so you shall be a blessing;
And I will bless those who bless you,
And the one who curses you I will curse
And in you all the families of the earth will be blessed."

Some consider this a prophecy of a savior.

So Abram went forth as the LORD had spoken
to him; and Lot went with him. Now Abram was
seventy-five years old when he departed from Haran.

Abram took Sarai his wife and Lot his nephew,
and all their possessions which they had accumulated,
and the persons which they had acquired in Haran, and
they set out for the land of Canaan; thus they came to
the land of Canaan.

Abram passed through the land as far as the site
of Shechem, to the oak of Moreh. Now the Canaanite
was then in the land.

The LORD appeared to Abram and said, "To
your descendants I will give this land."So he built an
altar there to the LORD who had appeared to him.

Then he proceeded from there to the mountain on the east of Bethel, and pitched his tent, with Bethel on the west and Ai on the east; and there he built an altar to the LORD and called upon the name of the LORD. Abram journeyed on, continuing toward the Negev.

Now there was a famine in the land; so Abram went down to Egypt to sojourn there, for the famine was severe in the land.

It came about when he came near to Egypt, that he said to Sarai his wife, "See now, I know that you are a beautiful woman; And when the Egyptians see you, they will say, 'This is his wife'; and they will kill me, but they will let you live.

"Please say that you are my sister so that it may go well with me because of you, and that I may live on account of you."

Even Abraham, God's chosen man, fudged a little to save his own hide. But Sarah actually was his half sister.

It came about when Abram came into Egypt, the Egyptians saw that the woman was very beautiful. Pharaoh's officials saw her and praised her to Pharaoh; and the woman was taken into Pharaoh's house. Therefore he treated Abram well for her sake; and gave him sheep and oxen and donkeys and male and female servants and female donkeys and camels.

But the LORD struck Pharaoh and his house with great plagues because of Sarai, Abram's wife.

Then Pharaoh called Abram and said, "What is this you have done to me? Why did you not tell me that she was your wife? "Why did you say, 'She is my sister,' so that I took her for my wife? Now then, here is your wife, take her and go."

Pharaoh commanded his men concerning him; and they escorted him away, with his wife and all that belonged to him. So Abram went up from Egypt to the

Negev, he and his wife and all that belonged to him, and Lot with him.

Now Abram was very rich in livestock, in silver and in gold. He went on his journeys from the Negev as far as Bethel, to the place where his tent had been at the beginning, between Bethel and Ai, to the place of the altar which he had made there formerly; and there Abram called on the name of the LORD.

Back to the similarities between the Israelites and early Americans, both Abraham's descendants and the American pioneers faced a hostile environment where there were already established tribes, Philistines and Native Americans, claiming the real estate. The Israelites were fierce fighters and claimed the Promised Land by killing off all of the inhabitants. While they followed God's commands, they succeeded.

We know that the American pioneers and U.S. Cavalry were unrelenting in their extermination of the Indians. It seemed that while the U.S. was God centered, it succeeded.

An 1899 chromolithograph of U.S. cavalry pursuing American Indians, artist unknown (Courtesy Wikipedia/Wikimedia)[72]

Eventually the Israelites decided to keep some of the spoils of their battles and a few select individuals whom they defeated, which was a violation of God's command. This may not be the only reason, but the survivors from Canaan contributed to the spread of idolatry through the Israelite community. As the idolatry spread, Israel fell from God's favor and suffered severe judgment time after time after time. Talk about slow learners.

I don't believe that the American pioneers picked up the spiritual values of the native American Indians, but over the years America, the great melting pot, has had a huge infusion of people of all faiths, and we even created a new religion right here in America. It seemed that the United States of America prospered greatly while it lived up to the motto on it's currency, "In God We Trust".

Kate Smith, An American Treasure
(Courtesy Wikipedia/Wikimedia)[73]

God Bless America is the beautiful song of blessing that Kate Smith would belt out over the airwaves. I wonder how she would sing that song today? "God-Ala-money-fame-porn-etc-etc-etc Bless

227

America, My Home, Sweet, Home, God-Ala-money-fame-porn-etc-etc-etc Bless America, My Home, Sweet, Home." It probably loses something in the translation, but I can hear it in my head. But I digress. While the United States remained grounded in it's Judeo-Christian values system, it plowed through hard times like depressions and wars, but still the U.S. was blessed.

I've been told many times that history repeats itself. My fear for America, that it also will face God's judgment, is partially based on a statement from President Obama. On the internet, http://www.huffingtonpost.com/2009/04/06/obama-us-not-a-christian_n_183772.html, the Huffington Post wrote:

> At a press conference in Turkey, President Obama casually rebuked the old chestnut that the United States is a Judeo-Christian nation.
> "One of the great strengths of the United States," the President said, "is ... we have a very large Christian population -- we do not consider ourselves a Christian nation or a Jewish nation or a Muslim nation. We consider ourselves a nation of citizens who are bound by ideals and a set of values."[257]

That statement, "we do not consider ourselves a Christian nation" was like a dagger. It seems like the Boy Scouts and a couple of churches are the only ones holding on to the original founding values of our country.

And what is an "old chestnut" anyway? An old chestnut is a frequently repeated joke or story or song.

I don't think the comment that "the United States is a Judeo-Christian nation" is a joke or a story. UNBELIEVABLE. Every history book I've ever read proves that the U.S. was based on Judeo-Christian law. And the laws when I grew up were basically don't lie, cheat, steal, or kill; Judeo-Christian concepts. But one of the most important things that I've learned over the years is that everything changes. Boy, did I ever grow up a sucker. I used to have faith in people. When I was young, I believed that a man said what he meant and meant what he said. Boy, has that ever changed. I'm not even going to start on that.

So I can't believe how far the United States has changed from the plan of the founding fathers. But history repeats itself and I should

228

not be surprised. It is all foretold in the Bible, but it sure is hard to watch.

The Bible explains what is happening in America like this: Bakers know the difference between leavened and unleavened bread. Leavened bread is bread that is made with yeast, which makes bread lighter and fluffier than flatbread. Yeast is a microscopic fungus that causes bread dough to "rise". My mom would get a "starter", which was some dough with yeast in it, and then she would make the BEST cinnamon rolls. She would mix up the new dough, add a little starter dough, cover it with a dishtowel and wait for it to rise. What made the dough rise, was, the yeast (fungus) in the "starter" would spread throughout the entire batch of dough through asexual reproduction and would ferment the carbohydrates which creates tiny carbon dioxide bubbles in the dough which makes the bread or pastry lighter and tastier. I remember as a high school freshman, we took an FFA project tour and Mom made those cinnamon rolls. Our ag teacher said they were the best he ever had. They were really good.

Yeast is mentioned in Mark 8.

> And they had forgotten to take bread, and did not have more than one loaf in the boat with them.
> And He was giving orders to them, saying, "Watch out! Beware of the leaven of the Pharisees and the leaven of Herod."
> They began to discuss with one another the fact that they had no bread.
> And Jesus, aware of this, said to them, "Why do you discuss the fact that you have no bread? Do you not yet see or understand? Do you have a hardened heart?
> "HAVING EYES, DO YOU NOT SEE? AND HAVING EARS, DO YOU NOT HEAR?

The leaven, or immorality, of the Pharisees is like the leaven of the entertainment business and the leaven of politicians and the leaven of business today. It is spread through the media, business organizations, and families, but it certainly doesn't make them better.

The Ol' Turkey Hunter

      The leaven that Jesus talked about worked the same way in his day as the leaven we have in America works today. Give immorality a little start and it spreads throughout the entire society.

      For the rest of the story, read in the middle of Genesis.

Tale #16
Blood

as told by

"The Ol' Turkey Hunter"

Shown here is Shaq and Pearl indicating that there was a pheasant just ahead of us. The Ol' Turkey Hunter took the picture and still got the pheasant.
Some people like different kinds of art, but for a hunter, a dog on point is a thing of intense beauty.

The Ol' Turkey Hunter

Blood

I thought that I was finished writing this book, but I didn't take my Tylenol PM today, and like I mentioned earlier, ideas just pop into my head. Most of my other ideas are for the next book if I write another one, but it seems that the idea that just hit me needs to be included here.

I really haven't had dreams that I remember since I changed blood pressure medicine four or five years ago, but I remember this one very clearly. I dreamed that I caught a big deer and had to subdue it. It got bloodier and bloodier before I woke up. For the next hour, I laid in bed thinking about blood, so let's see where this goes. I will apologize in advance for any graphic mental pictures to follow.

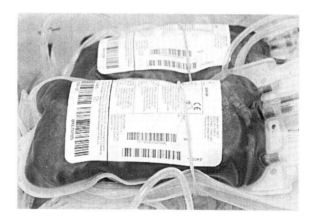

Bags of blood collected during donation, showing dark colour of venous blood.
User "montuno" on Flickr
(Courtesy Wikipedia/Wikimedia)[74]

Blood. Everyone knows about blood. Without blood, there is no life as we know it. Blood carries fuel that our bodies need, (oxygen, sugars, and other nutrients) to the muscles and other tissues and carries the waste away from the cells to the kidneys. Red Cross blood-drives tout giving blood as "give the gift of life".

Transfusions save thousands of lives each year. It's obvious, blood is an absolute basic necessity of multi-cellular life forms.

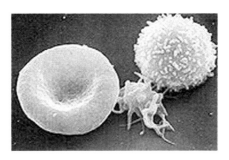

A scanning electron microscope (SEM) image of a normal red blood cell, a platelet, and a white blood cell.
(Courtesy Wikipedia/Wikimedia)[75]

Usually our first experience with blood is not a good one. It is usually our own blood and it usually involves pain and some sort of injury. I'm sure that I had other boo-boos when I was younger, but the first experience with blood that I remember came when I learned to ride my bike.

We lived on a gravel road that ran downhill for a quarter mile to the drop box where the ditch ran under the road. I got a 20 inch bicycle with fat tires but no training wheels and Dad would run along behind me holding me upright with his hand on the back of the seat and then give me a push to start me downhill. I would ride till I fell over. Then I would have to push the bike back up the hill (sometimes crying and picking the gravel out of my knee). I remember having bloody knees all that summer. It took a lot of spills and a lot of skin and blood before I got the hang of riding a bike.

The Drop Box
The drop box was a cement square where the water from the field
above dropped to go under the gravel road that went past our house.
It was a great place to play in the water and catch frogs and little
fish. I even caught a 2# catfish one time.
Photo by author.

I think a lot of times that people wince when blood is involved
because there is usually pain connected with the loss of blood. I hate
pain, my own and others. I don't exactly understand why.

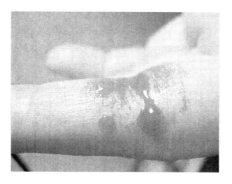

Capillary blood from a bleeding finger
Photo by Crystal (Crystl) from Bloomington, USA
(Courtesy Wikipedia/Wikimedia)[76]

Although some people claim to like pain (how can someone
like a toothache?????), pain is very important for our survival. Pain tells
us when something is wrong with our bodies, like gall bladder or

appendicitis, and pain sometimes warns us that we are in danger, like a broken bone. To avoid pain, we now have all kinds of medicines and anesthesia and pain killers that are such a blessing, but it hasn't always been that way.

Today, I think that people are so isolated from nature that they have lost their sense of reality. Recently I was talking with a young girl about 20 years old who made her dad stop hunting. When I questioned her, she said she loves KFC chicken, but she would never ever dress a chicken. She is very typical of many, many young people today. I thought to myself, if she lived 100 years ago she would clean a chicken and be thankful that she had a chicken to clean.

When I was a kid, dressing chickens was a big deal. We would catch the chickens the night before when they were roosting and easy to catch and put them in a cage. The next morning, Dad had a block of wood and he would chop off their heads with a hatchet and flip them on the ground where they would flop around like "a chicken with his head cut off". As the life giving blood drained out of the chickens, they would gradually quit flopping.

Grandpa Kerr had the water boiling and he would gather them up and dip the chickens in the boiling water so that we could pull out the feathers. Then Grandma Kerr would light a newspaper with a match, hold the featherless chicken by the legs, and singe any pin feathers off the carcass after we pulled out the big feathers. The coolest part was cleaning the gizzard. The gizzard, which most people consider a delicacy, is the muscle that grinds the food of birds since they have no teeth. I was always mesmerized when Grandma would cut the gizzard half way through, spread it open, and pull out the tissue lining, taking the undigested food and gravel out with it, all of this falling in an old steel bucket sitting on the kitchen floor. This sounds pretty sick, but it always happens in some form before you have gizzards to eat.

We never did this, but my eighth grade teacher told us that they used to take the feet they cut off the chickens and chase each other pulling the tendon so that the claws on the feet would open and close and grab at the person they were chasing. Again, an example of redneck recreation, but kids didn't have a Wii or a laptop computer or blood-and-guts video games to play with. Or even a gymnasium to play in. At my little school at Huntsville, we had to scoop the snow off of the finely ground limestone basketball court (not even blacktop) before we could play basketball in our coats, boots, and gloves. I don't know if kids could play under those conditions anymore.

A butcher's, Tacuinum sanitatis (a medieval handbook on wellness),casanatensis (XIV century) (Courtesy Wikipedia/Wikimedia)[77]

But today, almost all Americans are insulated from the unpleasantries of butchering and have little experience with large quantities of blood. We just go to the store and pick up a package of steaks or pork chops or chicken breasts. No blood, no guts, no stink, no effort.

Most people don't observe death anymore except what they see on TV and the movies, and it's about as real as the rest of the special effects they show. Death is not pretty.

Hollywood has cleaned up and glorified death, but the spirit or soul or whatever it is, doesn't give up as easily as it looks on TV. There is a phrase, "Give up the ghost". When an animal dies, you can usually tell when it "gives up the ghost", it usually involves severe thrashing and convulsing, a glazing over of the eyes, and I always find it very disagreeable.

A lot of people think that we should not eat meat and that's fine. Everyone is entitled to make their own choices and everyone can express their own opinion in our country as of today, but let's take a look at what the Bible says.

> And God blessed Noah and his sons and said
> to them, "Be fruitful and multiply, and fill the earth.
> "The fear of you and the terror of you will be
> on every beast of the earth and on every bird of the sky;
> with everything that creeps on the ground, and all the
> fish of the sea, into your hand they are given.
> "Every moving thing that is alive shall be food
> for you; I give all to you, as I gave the green plant.
> "Only you shall not eat flesh with its life, that is,
> its blood."

That's where kosher comes from. Wikipedia says that "Kosher foods are those that conform to the rules of Jewish religion. These rules form the main aspect of *kashrut*, Jewish dietary laws.

Reasons for food being non-kosher include the presence of ingredients derived from non-kosher animals or from kosher animals that were not properly slaughtered, a mixture of meat and milk, wine or grape juice (or their derivatives) produced without supervision, the use of produce from Israel that has not been tithed, or even the use of cooking utensils and machinery which had previously been used for non-kosher food.

One of the main biblical food laws is the forbidding of eating blood on account of the life [being] in the blood; this ban and reason are listed in the Noahide Laws, and twice in Leviticus, as well as by Deuteronomy The Priestly Code also prohibits the eating of fat, if it came from sacrificial land animals (cattle, sheep, and goats), since the fat is the portion of the meat exclusively allocated to YHWH (by burning it on the altar)."[77a]

"Life is in the blood". I believe that in more ways than one. Blood sacrifices were common in the old testament. That's probably not something that I'd think about doing in my spare time, so let's look at the origin of the practice.

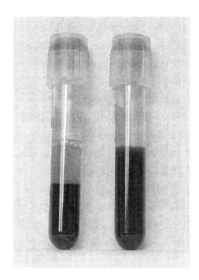

Two tubes of EDTA-anticoagulated blood.
Left tube: after standing, the RBCs have settled at the bottom of the
tube.
Right tube: contains freshly drawn blood.
(Courtesy Wikipedia/Wikimedia)[78]

Cain and Able were two of the first people to offer sacrifices.
Able's sacrifice, a lamb, was good and acceptable to God, but Cain's
sacrifice of grain was inferior to Able's.

> Now the man had relations with his wife Eve,
> and she conceived and gave birth to Cain, and she said,
> "I have gotten a manchild with the help of the LORD."
> Again, she gave birth to his brother Abel. And Abel
> was a keeper of flocks, but Cain was a tiller of the
> ground.
> So it came about in the course of time that Cain
> brought an offering to the LORD of the fruit of the
> ground. Abel, on his part also brought of the firstlings
> of his flock and of their fat portions And the LORD
> had regard for Abel and for his offering; but for Cain
> and for his offering He had no regard so Cain became
> very angry and his countenance fell.

Then the LORD said to Cain, "Why are you angry? And why has your countenance fallen? "If you do well, will not your countenance be lifted up? And if you do not do well, sin is crouching at the door; and its desire is for you, but you must master it."

Cain told Abel his brother. And it came about when they were in the field, that Cain rose up against Abel his brother and killed him. Then the LORD said to Cain, "Where is Abel your brother?" And he said, "I do not know. Am I my brother's keeper?"

He said, "What have you done? The voice of your brother's blood is crying to Me from the ground.

"Now you are cursed from the ground, which has opened its mouth to receive your brother's blood from your hand. When you cultivate the ground, it will no longer yield its strength to you; you will be a vagrant and a wanderer on the earth."

Cain said to the LORD, "My punishment is too great to bear! Behold, You have driven me this day from the face of the ground; and from Your face I will be hidden, and I will be a vagrant and a wanderer on the earth, and whoever finds me will kill me."

So the LORD said to him, "Therefore whoever kills Cain, vengeance will be taken on him sevenfold " And the LORD appointed a sign for Cain, so that no one finding him would slay him.

Then Cain went out from the presence of the LORD, and settled in the land of Nod, east of Eden.

So I have to wonder why a lamb is an acceptable sacrifice while grain, also the fruit of his labor, was unacceptable. Well, let's look back at Cain and Able's parents.

Now the serpent was more crafty than any beast of the field which the LORD God had made. And he said to the woman, "Indeed, has God said, 'You shall not eat from any tree of the garden'?"

The woman said to the serpent, "From the fruit of the trees of the garden we may eat; But from the fruit of the tree which is in the middle of the garden, God has said, 'You shall not eat from it or touch it, or you will die.'"

The serpent said to the woman, "You surely will not die! For God knows that in the day you eat from it your eyes will be opened, and you will be like God, knowing good and evil."

When the woman saw that the tree was good for food, and that it was a delight to the eyes, and that the tree was desirable to make one wise, she took from its fruit and ate; and she gave also to her husband with her, and he ate. Then the eyes of both of them were opened, and they knew that they were naked; and they sewed fig leaves together and made themselves loin coverings.

They heard the sound of the LORD God walking in the garden in the cool of the day, and the man and his wife hid themselves from the presence of the LORD God among the trees of the garden. Then the LORD God called to the man, and said to him, "Where are you?"

He said, "I heard the sound of You in the garden, and I was afraid because I was naked; so I hid myself."

And He said, "Who told you that you were naked? Have you eaten from the tree of which I commanded you not to eat?"

The man said, "The woman whom You gave to be with me, she gave me from the tree, and I ate."

Then the LORD God said to the woman, "What is this you have done?" And the woman said, "The serpent deceived me, and I ate."

The LORD God said to the serpent,
"Because you have done this,
Cursed are you more than all cattle,
And more than every beast of the field;
On your belly you will go,
And dust you will eat

The Ol' Turkey Hunter

All the days of your life;
And I will put enmity
Between you and the woman,
And between your seed and her seed;
He shall bruise you on the head,
And you shall bruise him on the heel."
     To the woman He said,
"I will greatly multiply
Your pain in childbirth,
In pain you will bring forth children;
Yet your desire will be for your husband,
And he will rule over you."
     Then to Adam He said,
"Because you have listened to the voice of your wife,
and have eaten from the tree about which I
commanded you, saying, 'You shall not eat from it';
Cursed is the ground because of you;
In toil you will eat of it
All the days of your life.
"Both thorns and thistles it shall grow for you;
And you will eat the plants of the field;
By the sweat of your face
You will eat bread,
Till you return to the ground,
Because from it you were taken;
For you are dust,
And to dust you shall return."
     Now the man called his wife's name Eve,
because she was the mother of all the living.
     The LORD God made garments of skin for
Adam and his wife, and clothed them.

So God made clothes out of animal skins for Adam and Eve. Animals don't give up their skins easily. That means they died to give up their hides which were used to cover up man's sin. So, actually, the animals, probably lambs, shed their blood, which earlier we said was it's life, to cover mans' sin, that's blood sacrifices, a common theme throughout the Old Testament.

While the Israelites were wondering in the desert near Mt. Sinai, this happened.

Then He said to Moses, "Come up to the LORD, you and Aaron, Nadab and Abihu and seventy of the elders of Israel, and you shall worship at a distance.

"Moses alone, however, shall come near to the LORD, but they shall not come near, nor shall the people come up with him."

Then Moses came and recounted to the people all the words of the LORD and all the ordinances; and all the people answered with one voice and said, "All the words which the LORD has spoken we will do!"

Moses wrote down all the words of the LORD. Then he arose early in the morning, and built an altar at the foot of the mountain with twelve pillars for the twelve tribes of Israel.

He sent young men of the sons of Israel, and they offered burnt offerings and sacrificed young bulls as peace offerings to the LORD.

Moses took half of the blood and put it in basins, and the other half of the blood he sprinkled on the altar.

Then he took the book of the covenant and read it in the hearing of the people; and they said, "All that the LORD has spoken we will do, and we will be obedient!"

So Moses took the blood and sprinkled it on the people, and said, "Behold the blood of the covenant, which the LORD has made with you in accordance with all these words."

Then Moses went up with Aaron, Nadab and Abihu, and seventy of the elders of Israel,

And they saw the God of Israel; and under His feet there appeared to be a pavement of sapphire, as clear as the sky itself.

Yet He did not stretch out His hand against the nobles of the sons of Israel; and they saw God, and they ate and drank.

YUCK!!!! I don't want anyone sprinkling blood on me. What a nasty, sticky mess. But this is symbolic of God forgiving our sins and reestablishing our close relationship with Him. I think the act of sacrificing animals became too ritualistic and legalistic. Slaughtering a sheep for this and a goat for that and a dove for this and a bull for that. Finally a perfect blood sacrifice was offered to end all sacrifices.

For the Law, since it has only a shadow of the good things to come and not the very form of things, can never, by the same sacrifices which they offer continually year by year, make perfect those who draw near.

Otherwise, would they not have ceased to be offered, because the worshipers, having once been cleansed, would no longer have had consciousness of sins?

But in those sacrifices there is a reminder of sins year by year. For it is impossible for the blood of bulls and goats to take away sins.

Therefore, when He comes into the world, He says,"SACRIFICE AND OFFERING YOU HAVE NOT DESIRED, BUT A BODY YOU HAVE PREPARED FOR ME; IN WHOLE BURNT OFFERINGS AND SACRIFICES FOR SIN YOU HAVE TAKEN NO PLEASURE.

"THEN I SAID, 'BEHOLD, I HAVE COME (IN THE SCROLL OF THE BOOK IT IS WRITTEN OF ME) TO DO YOUR WILL, O GOD.'"

After saying above, "SACRIFICES AND OFFERINGS AND WHOLE BURNT OFFERINGS AND SACRIFICES FOR SIN YOU HAVE NOT DESIRED, NOR HAVE YOU TAKEN PLEASURE IN THEM" (which are offered according to the Law),

Then He said, "BEHOLD, I HAVE COME TO DO YOUR WILL." He takes away the first in order to establish the second. (*I believe this refers to abolishment of the previous covenant and establishment of the current covenant with God*).

By this will we have been sanctified through the offering of the body of Jesus Christ once for all.

Every priest stands daily ministering and offering time after time the same sacrifices, which can never take away sins; but He, having offered one sacrifice for sins for all time, SAT DOWN AT THE RIGHT HAND OF GOD, waiting from that time onward UNTIL HIS ENEMIES BE MADE A FOOTSTOOL FOR HIS FEET.

For by one offering He has perfected for all time those who are sanctified. And the Holy Spirit also testifies to us; for after saying, "THIS IS THE COVENANT THAT I WILL MAKE WITH THEM AFTER THOSE DAYS, SAYS THE LORD: I WILL PUT MY LAWS UPON THEIR HEART, AND ON THEIR MIND I WILL WRITE THEM,"

He then says, "AND THEIR SINS AND THEIR LAWLESS DEEDS I WILL REMEMBER NO MORE."

Now where there is forgiveness of these things, there is no longer any offering for sin.

Israelites started offering blood sacrifices almost at the beginning of time, but according to the Dake's Annotated Reference Bible, page 259, "…Christ has come to do away with the sin-offerings of the Mosaic system by His one offering which cleanses from all sin. It is a historical fact that after Christ died the sacrifices of the law ceased. Jews have had no sacrifices for 1900 years (Hos.3:4-5)

So it looks like a sacrifice to end all sacrifices occurred about 0 BC. And to get back to the subject of blood, in that final sacrifice there was bloodshed. This is how the Bible explains it.

Then the Jews, because it was the day of preparation, so that the bodies would not remain on the cross on the Sabbath (for that Sabbath was a high day), asked Pilate that their legs might be broken, and that they might be taken away.

So the soldiers came, and broke the legs of the first man and of the other who was crucified with Him; but coming to Jesus, when they saw that He was already dead, they did not break His legs. But one of the soldiers pierced His side with a spear, and immediately blood and water came out.

The First Good Friday
(Courtesy Wikipedia/Wikimedia)[79]

And he who has seen has testified, and his testimony is true; and he knows that he is telling the truth, so that you also may believe. For these things came to pass to fulfill the Scripture, "NOT A BONE OF HIM SHALL BE BROKEN." And again another Scripture says, "THEY SHALL LOOK ON HIM WHOM THEY PIERCED."

And that leads to another story, but we'll save that for another day.

Tale #17
Things Change
as told by
"The Ol' Turkey Hunter"
Shown here as a picture family tree.

The Ol' Turkey Hunter

Things Change

Everything changes. I've always lived in western Illinois and people have always said that "if you don't like the weather now, just wait a couple of hours". Well, the weather can change very quickly, and when it does, it usually results in some type of hazardous weather conditions, but the weather isn't the only thing to change around here.

Things change so dramatically today that I can't keep up with the changes, but I think that my grandparents saw some of the most dramatic changes in history. If I can figure backward, I think that Grandpa Kerr was born in 1910 and Grandpa Janssen was born in 1899. Grandpa Janssen died in the 1990's, so let's look at some of the changes he saw.

A horse and buggy circa 1910
(Courtesy Wikipedia/Wikimedia)[80]

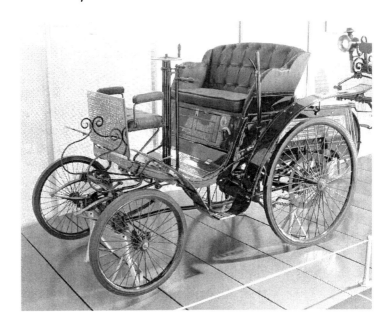

Karl Benz's "Velo" model (1894) - entered into an
early automobile race
(Courtesy Wikipedia/Wikimedia)[81]

When my Grandpa, August, was a child, transportation was by horse and buggy. The wagons and buggies had high steel wheels so that the horses could pull their loads over dirt roads that often times had very deep, muddy ruts carved into them. That really limited the distances traveled by people of that time period.

Jump forward to 1990. A 1990 Oldsmobile or Cadillac, although not nearly as nice as the vehicles we enjoy today, was a pretty nice ride.

As you can tell from these pictures, the changes in personal transportation that my grandparents experienced were enormous.

The hydrogen powered FCHV (Fuel Cell Hybrid Vehicle) was developed by Toyota in 2005

Wikipedia says, "TOYOTA FCHV(Fuel Cell Hybrid Vehicle). The fuel cell hybrid car which runs from the hydrogen which Toyota Motor developed. Toyota FCHV which took a photograph is one of the sets which has only 12 sets in the Japan and the U.S. which Nagoya-shi is using as a public vehicle. The contributor took a photograph by taking an appointment to the Nagoya environmental office."

Photo by Gnsin

(Courtesy Wikipedia/Wikimedia)[82]

Many people today are nostalgic about the olden days of railroads when people rode in passenger cars pulled by the old steam engines puffing and smoking down the tracks, but most people today don't have the time to leisurely cruise on the rails to their destination. Amtrak makes multiple trips today between towns because people got things to do and are always in a hurry.

Steam locomotive-hauled passenger train.
(c) Mike Crowe
Saturday, 26 March, 2005
(Courtesy Wikipedia/Wikimedia)[83]

German ICE high speed passenger train (a form of multiple unit)
I don't know how fast this train runs, probably over 100 mph,
but I'd hate to see a dog or cow that got in it's way.
Photo by Sebastian Terfloth
(Courtesy Wikipedia/Wikimedia)[84]

Illustration of mythological beings Icarus and Daedalus attempting
to fly using wax wings.
(Courtesy Wikipedia/Wikimedia)[85]

People have always dreamed of flying like a bird. Wikipedia
says that "According to the Smithsonian Institution and Federation
Aeronautique Internationale (FAI), the Wrights made the first
sustained, controlled, powered heavier-than-air manned flight at Kill
Devil Hills, North Carolina, four miles (8 km) south of Kitty Hawk,
North Carolina on December 17, 1903."

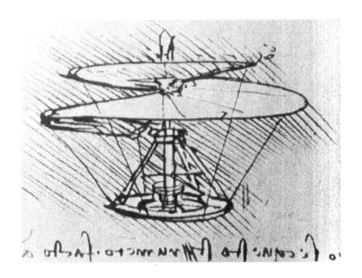

Leonardo da Vinci's "aerial screw" design.
(Courtesy Wikipedia/Wikimedia)[86]

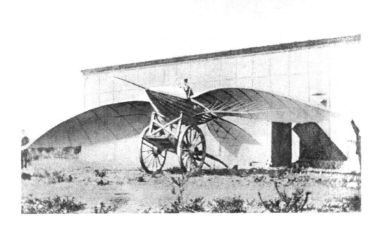

Jean-Marie Le Bris and his flying machine, Albatros II, 1868.
(Courtesy Wikipedia/Wikimedia)[87]

The Wright Flyer: the first sustained flight with a powered,
controlled aircraft.
(Courtesy Wikipedia/Wikimedia)[88]

"The first flight by Orville Wright, of 120 feet (37 m) in 12
seconds, was recorded in a famous photograph. In the fourth flight
of the same day, Wilbur Wright flew 852 feet (260 m) in 59 seconds.
The flights were witnessed by three coastal lifesaving crewmen, a
local businessman, and a boy from the village, making these the first
public flights and the first well-documented ones." [88]

And air travel was limited to birds and bats. I don't think the
Wright brothers flew until the 20th century. Look at where space travel
has gone since then; to the moon and past. People living when
Abraham Lincoln was alive could not even imagine some of the
changes, but there seems to be a rule that everything changes.

A Concorde Jet
Wikipedia says, "Concorde G-BOAB in storage at London
Heathrow Airport following the end of all Concorde flying. This
aircraft flew for 22,296 hours between its first flight in 1976 and its
final flight in 2000."
(Courtesy Wikipedia/Wikimedia)[89]

It seems that I have a hard time adjusting to all of these
changes. I have to get my grandchildren to set my watch and the clock
in my car. I can mess and mess with my watch and not figure out
anything, but they just take it and "do-do-do-do......here you go,
Grandpa." How do they do that?

An abacus from a Danish elementary school. Early 20th century.
Size: 40 cm wide, 46 cm high.
My Grandpa's Computer
(Courtesy Wikipedia/Wikimedia)[90]

And computers. I think that everything electronic hates me.
The computer just bleep, bleep, bleep, really frustrates me sometimes,
and my cell phone, I don't know why it won't do what I want it to do.
My printer won't work right now because I just had to get my
computer dumped and I can't find the disk with the driver program to
reload it.

Apollo 11 lifts off on its mission to land a man on the moon
(Courtesy Wikipedia/Wikimedia)[91]

And last night I burned up a plastic plate in the microwave because I tried to zap a potato for 3:33 and the plate wouldn't take it. I switched plates, finished zapping it, and ate the potato anyway.

And I have to use two remotes for the TV and cable and the DVD player because I'm not smart enough to figure out how to program the universal remote and then I can't find the remote that I need when I need it. Often times I even have to get up out of my chair to get the remote to change the channel. Is that aggravating!!! Grandpa Kerr and Grandpa Janssen didn't have to mess with any of that stuff, but they did have to get up to change the channel on the TV, course they only had two channels to choose from. So maybe they would have had just as hard a time adjusting to the changes in the world as I'm having, but they just weren't exposed to as many changes as I'm experiencing.

Back to the rule that everything changes. There are lots of rules that we learn about. How about the rule of spelling that states "I before E, except after C"? If I remember back to the old Huntsville Grade School, we spelled "relieve" with the IE vowels in that order, but we spelled "receive" with the IE vowels in reverse order because of the exception to the spelling rule.

As I go through life, it seems that there are lots of rules, but then there is always an exception to each of those rules. I've heard it said that all rules and records are made to be broken.

So in my life, my family has grown, my jobs change, my home has changed, I live in a different town, my appearance has changed, my pets have changed, my doctors have changed, my friends have changed, my thinking has changed, my tastes have changed, my politics have changed, my vehicles have changed, my hair has fallen out and turned grey, my waist has expanded, everything in my life has changed.

But like I mentioned earlier, I've found that there is an exception to every rule, including the rule that everything changes, and this is the Biblical exception:

Jesus Christ is the same yesterday and today and forever.

The Ol' Turkey Hunter

The Parable
of the Turkey Hunter

Like I mentioned in the book, the reason for the book was to promote a presentation that I've been given called <u>The Parable of the Turkey Hunter</u>. It's kind of like the movies that start out the same, but you can choose different endings.

The program includes many different animal calls and the equipment that is used by turkey hunters in their quest to subdue a turkey gobbler.

Turkey gobbles, squawks, yelps, and putts are heard intermingled with hoot owl hoots, crow calls, and deer grunts. I just bought an elk call to include in the program. That purchase almost got me in trouble.

I ordered the elk call from Cabela's on December 15th over the internet. $34.99 plus $8.95 shipping and $2.19 tax for a total of $46.13. I casually mentioned to Katie that I'd made an order over the internet, but she already knew about it because it showed up on the bank statement. Kind of excited or hopeful, she asked if it was for her Christmas present. I had to hang my head when I disappointed her with the news that it wasn't. Hopefully, I made a good recovery when I brought home some honey sausage links and hash browns and cinnamon rolls and orange juice and made her breakfast two days later.

But back to the presentation, the first part demonstrates the tactics that are used by turkey hunters to fool a turkey into his untimely demise, tactics that include false turkey conversations, a love triangle, concealment, and plastic reproductions.

After everyone understands the concepts of turkey hunting, this is where the parable part comes in. A parable is a story about something simple, something that is easy to understand, that helps us understand a more complex concept.

The unique part of <u>The Parable of the Turkey Hunter</u> is that the parable can be adjusted to fit the audience. The turkey hunter uses many tricks to fool the turkey so that he can kill and destroy the turkey. The parallel is that the devil or negative forces or whatever fools us in many ways to destroy our peace, our joy, and our hope. But different tricks are used on different groups of people.

Older folks are fooled by the tricks of loneliness and discouragement. The Parable for older seniors addresses the cycle of life and helps them realize that they are valuable to their friends and family, to theirselves, and to their maker.

The Parable in youth and general audiences addresses the tricks of guilt and shame. It explains how everyone carries the burdens of guilt and shame to some extent which undermines the well-being of each individual. Steals their peace, hope, and joy.

For Boy Scouts, it reinforces the values of the Boy Scout Law and also addresses the pitfalls of drug use for young people.

At Father-Son banquets, three keys to being a good father are the focal point.

I am still formulating a program for the school system. I have been certified as an Illinois State Board of Education Approved Professional Provider, #090625112221037.

There may be more themes in the future, but these have been very well received in the past.

If anyone would like to have an entertaining speaker that will hold everyone's attention for a full hour and have an impact upon the rest of their lives, you can contact me at kerrsetters@hotmail.com.

I hope that you have found this book to be entertaining, enlightening, and thought provoking; and I hope that you feel free to explore the Bible more deeply. There's lots more good stuff in it.

Addresses for web pictures included.

[1]http://en.wikipedia.org/wiki/File:WPA_Outhouse.jpg

[2]http://en.wikipedia.org/wiki/File:Hooper-Bowler-Hillstrom_House2.JPG

[3]http://en.wikipedia.org/wiki/File:Ark_of_the_Covenant_19th-century.png

[4]http://en.wikipedia.org/wiki/Dagon

[5]http://en.wikipedia.org/wiki/File:Bullock_cart_in_Tamil_Nadu.jpg

[6]http://commons.wikimedia.org/wiki/File:Cow_and_calf.jpg

[7]http://en.wikipedia.org/wiki/Headless_Horseman

[8]http://commons.wikimedia.org/wiki/File:Bette_Davis_in_Jezebel_trailer.jpg

[9]http://en.wikipedia.org/wiki/File:Drought.jpg

[10]http://en.wikipedia.org/wiki/File:Cloud_Seeding.svg

[11]http://en.wikipedia.org/wiki/File:Krunkwerke_-_IMG_4515_(by-sa).jpg

[12]http://en.wikipedia.org/wiki/File:LightningStruckTree.png

[13]http://en.wikipedia.org/wiki/File:Sts8storm.jpg

[14]http://en.wikipedia.org/wiki/File:The_Death_of_Jezebel.jpg

[15]http://science.hq.nasa.gov/kids/imagers/ems/visible.html

[16]http://science.hq.nasa.gov/kids/imagers/ems/visible.html[16]

[17]http://www.google.com/imgres?imgurl=http://upload.wiki
media.org/wikipedia/commons/f/f7/BenjaminWest-Saul-and-
the-Witch-of-Endor-
1777.jpg&imgrefurl=http://commons.wikimedia.org/wiki/Fil
e:BenjaminWest-Saul-and-the-Witch-of-
Endor1777.jpg&h=583&w=765&sz=97&tbnid=wvbnFVya3
w6ndM:&tbnh=108&tbnw=142&prev=/images%3Fq%3Dwi
tch%2Bof%2Bendor&usg=__dEBncZRVAgjhw43eePbpjG
Dh7m8=&ei=VsfASs2lBpWn8AaG6PmlAQ&sa=X&oi=ima
ge_result&resnum=6&ct=image

[18]http://en.wikipedia.org/wiki/File:
Louvre_rosa_apparition.jpg

[19]http://en.wikipedia.org/wiki/Belshazzar

[20]http://en.wikipedia.org/wiki/File:Bascula_9.jpg

[21]http://en.wikipedia.org/wiki/Shekel

[22]http://en.wikipedia.org/wiki/File:Leprosy.jpg

[23]http://en.wikipedia.org/wiki/File:CornShocksForestvilleMi
nnesota2006.JPG

[24]http://en.wikipedia.org/wiki/Joseph_(Hebrew_Bible)

[25]http://en.wikipedia.org/wiki/Faience

[26]http://www.thepigpage.com/Gerth/images/2008/08-06/2nd-Round-
Show-Pigs-022.jpg

[27]http://www.thepigpage.com/Gerth/index.html

[28]www.mcdonoughvoice.com

[29]http://en.wikipedia.org/wiki/File:Roasted_chicken.jpg

[30]http://en.wikipedia.org/wiki/File:Chicken_eggs.jpg

[31]http://en.wikipedia.org/wiki/File:Buff_Orpington_Chick.jpg

[32]www.stevenspoultryfarm.com

[33]http://www.thepigpage.com/Gerth/images/2008/08-28/Pig-Pictures-002.jpg

[34]http://en.wikipedia.org/wiki/File:Sperm-egg.jpg

[35]http://en.wikipedia.org/wiki/File:Intel_4004.jpg

[36]http://en.wikipedia.org/wiki/Ouija

[37]http://en.wikipedia.org/wiki/File:RogerTractorLarge.jpg

[38]

[39]http://news.webshots.com/album/559194245Erfyce

[40]

[41]http://en.wikipedia.org/wiki/Garden_of_Eden

[42]http://commons.wikimedia.org/wiki/File:Big_bang.jpg

[43]http://en.wikipedia.org/wiki/Big_Bang

[44]http://en.wikipedia.org/wiki/Adam_and_Eve

[45]http://en.wikipedia.org/wiki/Adam_and_Eves_Cranach_d._%C3%84._001.jpg

[46]http://en.wikipedia.org/wiki/Donkey

[47]http://en.wikipedia.org/wiki/Mule

[48]http://en.wikipedia.org/wiki/Donkey_basketball

[49]http://commons.wikimedia.org/wiki/File:Palomino_Horse.jp

[50]http://en.wikipedia.org/wiki/File:Rembrandt_Harmensz._van_Rijn_122.jpg

[51]http://en.wikipedia.org/wiki/File:Religion-Pearce-Highsmith-detail-1.jpeg

[52]http://en.wikipedia.org/wiki/Baal

[53]http://en.wikipedia.org/wiki/File:Merino_shearing.jpg

[54]Found on lavistachurchofchrist.org

[55]http://en.wikipedia.org/wiki/File:PLATE4DX.jpg

[56]http://en.wikipedia.org/wiki/Beach_volleyball

[57]http://en.wikipedia.org/wiki/File:Lazarus_Bethany.JP

[58]http://en.wikipedia.org/wiki/File:Vincent_Van_Gogh_La_R%C3%A9surrection_de_Lazare_(d%E2%80%99apr%C3%A8s_Rembrandt).JP

[59]http://en.wikipedia.org/wiki/File:%D0%92%D0%BE%D1%81%D0%BA%D1%80%D0%B5%D1%88%D0%B5%D0%BD%D0%B8%D0%B5_%D0%9B%D0%B0%D0%B7%D0%B0%D1%80%D1%8F.jpg

[60]http://en.wikipedia.org/wiki/File:1867_Edward_Poynter_-_Israel_in_Egypt.jpg

[61]http://en.wikipedia.org/wiki/File:Ruebens_massacre.jpg

[62]http://en.wikipedia.org/wiki/File:MtSinaiPano.jpg

[63]http://en.wikipedia.org/wiki/File:Rembrandt_Harmensz._va n_Rijn_079.jpg

[64]http://en.wikipedia.org/wiki/File:Dszpics1.jpg

[65]http://en.wikipedia.org/wiki/Samuel_(Bible)

[66]http://en.wikipedia.org/wiki/File:Gerbrand_van_den_Eeckh out_-Anna_toont_haar_zoon_Samu %C3%ABl_aan_de_priester_Eli.jpg

[67]http://en.wikipedia.org/wiki/File:Rey_David_por_Pedro_B erruguete.JPG

[68]http://en.wikipedia.org/wiki/File:Statue_of_Liberty_April_2008.JP G

[69]http://en.wikipedia.org/wiki/File:Truth.jpg

[70]http://en.wikipedia.org/wiki/File:Nancy_Reagan_reopens_Statue_o f_Liberty_1986.jpg

[71]http://jwa.org/exhibits/wov/lazarus/el9.html
<http://jwa.org/exhibits/wov/lazarus/el9.html> (October 8, 2009).

[72]http://en.wikipedia.org/wiki/File:Cavalry_and_Indians.JPG

[73]http://katesmith.org/

[74]http://en.wikipedia.org/wiki/File:Bloodbags.jpg

[75]http://en.wikipedia.org/wiki/Blood

[76]http://en.wikipedia.org/wiki/File:Bleeding_finger.jpg

[77]http://en.wikipedia.org/wiki/File:11-alimenti,carni_ovine, Taccuino_Sanitatis,_Casanatense_4182.jpg

[77a]http://en.wikipedia.org/wiki/Kosher

[78]http://en.wikipedia.org/wiki/Blood

[79]http://en.wikipedia.org/wiki/File:

[80]http://en.wikipedia.org/wiki/File:Horse_and_buggy_1910.jpg

[81]http://en.wikipedia.org/wiki/Automobile

[82]http://en.wikipedia.org/wiki/File:TOYOTA_FCHV_01.jpg

[83]http://en.wikipedia.org/wiki/File:5051_Earl_Bathurst_Cocklewood_Harbour.jpg

[84]http://en.wikipedia.org/wiki/File:ICE_3_Fahlenbach.jpg

[85]http://en.wikipedia.org/wiki/File:Landon-IcarusandDaedalus.jpg

[86]http://en.wikipedia.org/wiki/File:Leonardo_da_Vinci_helicopter.jpg

[87]http://en.wikipedia.org/wiki/Aviation_history